REUNITED WITH HER SECRET PRINCE

SUSANNE HAMPTON

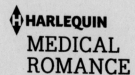

HARLEQUIN

MEDICAL
ROMANCE

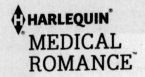

HARLEQUIN®
MEDICAL
ROMANCE™

Recycling programs
for this product may
not exist in your area.

ISBN-13: 978-1-335-40431-2

Reunited with Her Secret Prince

Harlequin Enterprises ULC
22 Adelaide St. West, 40th Floor
Toronto, Ontario M5H 4E3, Canada
www.Harlequin.com

Printed in U.S.A.

Married to the man she met at eighteen, **Susanne Hampton** is the mother of two adult daughters, Orianthi and Tina. She has enjoyed a varied career path but finally found her way to her favorite role of all: Harlequin Medical Romance author. Susanne has always read romance novels and says, "I love a happy-ever-after, so writing for Harlequin is a dream come true."

Books by Susanne Hampton

Harlequin Medical Romance

Christmas Miracles in Maternity
White Christmas for the Single Mom

The Monticello Baby Miracles
Twin Surprise for the Single Doc

Midwives On-Call
Midwife's Baby Bump

Unlocking the Doctor's Heart
Back in Her Husband's Arms
Falling for Dr. December
A Baby to Bind Them
A Mommy to Make Christmas
The Doctor's Cinderella
Mending the Single Dad's Heart

Visit the Author Profile page at Harlequin.com.

To my amazing family and friends who have
supported and encouraged my writing journey…
and unknowingly given me the most wonderful
inspiration for my characters.

PROLOGUE

It WAS THE twelfth of June, a perfect summer's day in the northern hemisphere, and one that nurse Libby McDonald would never forget.

It was the day her life changed for ever. Perched precariously on the edge of her bed, she struggled to fill her lungs with air as her emotions threatened to overwhelm her. Her life was suddenly spinning out of control and Libby was powerless to change anything, which was completely at odds with her character. She was, without exception, calm even in the most stressful times but this was not Cardiology or the ER and she was not triaging patients; she was suddenly trying to triage her escalating fears. And failing miserably.

Her emerald green eyes darted from the test results to the floor and back again as her fingers nervously tapped on the side of her bed, making a sound barely audible above the beating of her heart. It was as though if she didn't stare too long in the direction of the test strip, it wouldn't be real. But it was real. There were no faint lines. There was no ambiguity about it. Libby was going to have the baby of the man who had exited her life as mysteriously as he had entered it.

The boldness of the two lines on the pregnancy test were almost screaming the result at her.

And reminding her of her poor judgement when she fell in love so quickly and realised in hindsight that while she had thought he was everything she was looking for and more, she had fallen in love with a man she really didn't know at all.

Her life would most definitely be nothing close to the 'white picket fence' perfect one that she had imagined. The one where she was happily married to the man of her dreams, living in a rustic cottage by the ocean with a baby on the way. In reality, while Libby had a baby on the way, she was renting a condo in Oakland, about 20 minutes from San Francisco and not not too far from her retired parents. And she was still paying off her student loan while trying to save for a car to replace the ageing one in the driveway.

There was nothing perfect about her life in her mind, at least not any more. Less than two months earlier she had thought it was as perfect as any woman could dream possible when she'd unexpectedly found herself falling in love. He was a six-foot-two dark-haired, handsome and charismatic doctor and they had been working together at the hospital for almost a month when she had taken a leap of faith and changed their relationship status from colleagues to lovers by inviting him home late one night. While it had been out of character for Libby since they hadn't been actually dating, it had felt right.

They had spent many hours working together in ER and they had been sharing lunch whenever possible and having lengthy discussions about their mutual love of medicine over late-night coffee when ER was quiet and they could steal away to the twenty-four-hour cafeteria. He had encouraged Libby to consider specialising in Cardiology when she'd told him how much she enjoyed rotations in that department and he had gone so far as to find out the next study intake for her.

She had tried to hide her growing feelings for him but at times that had been almost impossible. Observing him with patients, many seen under extreme duress, Libby's admiration had grown by the day. He had been equally as kind and caring as he was thorough and responsive, and she had watched as his knowledge and experience had changed the outcomes for many critically ill patients. Her professional respect had blossomed into something so much more.

Libby could not help but notice that his demeanour had seemed a little sombre and distant at times, but his mood had always seemed to lift when he'd seen her and she'd felt like she was floating whenever he was around.

She had only dated two men before him, one just out of college for a year before they'd both realised they were better off as friends and then there had been another six-month relationship with a medical student that had been set up by their mothers. When it had ended it had broken their respective mothers' hearts but not their own. And neither relationship had been overly passionate, closer to lukewarm, so she had decided to concentrate on her studies and her career.

But that fateful night when she had acted on her growing feelings, he had made her believe she was the only woman in the world. The way he'd held her and made love to her had made her naively trust that he was the man who would love her for ever. As she'd lain in the warmth of his tender embrace, with the dappled moonlight shining through the open drapes, listening to him gently sleeping, she'd hoped that since they had crossed over from colleagues to lovers, she would learn more about his life outside the hospital and over time something of his family, his past and his dreams for the future.

Libby had thought in her heart she had found *the one*.

But the opportunity to learn anything about him outside medicine had never come as the next morning she had awoken to find him gone. His side of her bed had been cold and empty and she'd soon learned the devastating truth that he had left town. He had given notice at the hospital that morning via email and disappeared. Very quickly she'd discovered he was not *the one*.

Almost eight weeks later she was facing the biggest challenge of her twenty-nine years and the fact that the one night they had shared had changed her life from nurse to single mother despite them taking precautions. There would be no better half to help her. No partner to share the joy and the pain.

Libby no longer cared to know anything about the man, his life or his past. What she did know was that she would have to face this alone and she also knew that she could never again allow her emotions to cloud her judgement. And never let her heart rule her head.

Collapsing back across the bed and staring at the ceiling fan as it slowly made circles in the warm air, Libby couldn't pretend, even to herself, to be surprised by the confirmation of her pregnancy. Her hands instinctively covered her stomach. There was no physical sign but in her heart she was already protective of her baby. Even in the pharmacy as she'd purchased the test that afternoon, she'd thought her action was redundant.

She had been feeling nauseous for almost six weeks and she had eaten more olives, fish and bread than she cared to remember in the preceding days. Which for anyone else might not be odd, except Libby detested olives. But, like a woman possessed, she had driven to the late-night supermarket close to midnight in search of black olives. They had to be Kalamata olives. And artisan bread. And that week she had started visiting the fish market and she ordinarily hated the smell of fresh fish.

Her cravings were Mediterranean, just like the father of her unborn child. The man who had shattered her heart and her trust.

Suddenly, there was a knock on the front

door, breaking through the jumbled thoughts that were threatening to send her mad.

'Hello…anyone gorgeous at home? Other than me, I mean?' the voice chirped loudly.

She recognised the voice of her best friend, Bradley. The rock in her life since nursing school. She had been expecting him but was clueless as to how he would react as he hadn't known she had even been interested in someone and Libby had never kept secrets from Bradley. Slowly she sat up and then climbed to her feet. Her legs were still shaking and her mind racing.

'The door's unlocked and I'm in my room, Bradley… There's something I need to tell you.'

Thirty minutes later, they both sat staring in silence at their empty iced tea glasses. Bradley had moved Libby into the kitchen and insisted that she have a cool drink and something to eat. He had brought home two cupcakes from the local bakery and there were now only crumbs on their plates. She suspected that he needed something to calm his nerves as much as her. Learning about her pregnancy had come out of left field for him.

'He's a lying, deceitful bastard on every level.'

'I feel so stupid. I mean, I didn't really know him, not outside work, but we just clicked. We talked for hours literally and it seemed right. But it was so wrong. And I don't have that much dating experience, not in last few years anyway. I guess I read too much into it.'

'He clearly wanted you to read into it. He's a dreadful excuse for a man.'

'I'm an idiot.'

Bradley patted her hand with his. 'You're not an idiot. Love just makes us do crazy things. Heaven knows, I've fallen for the wrong man more times than I care to recall.'

Libby nodded. She was done with talking about the man who had broken her heart. And there would be no more tears either. She had shed enough in the weeks since he'd left to last her a lifetime and now she needed to focus on herself. And her baby.

'I know it's a lot but *we've* got this,' he said with his chin definitely jutted and his hands on his hips. 'I'm in this with you, all the way.'

'That's so sweet, Bradley, but I made a mess of everything. Not you. You've got a whole wide world out there. You don't have to tie yourself down to me and...' Libby paused as her gaze dropped to her stomach. 'And my baby.'

'What sort of gay best friend walks away from his best friend for ever and her baby? Not me, that's for sure,' he retorted, standing and reaching for both cups. He walked to the dishwasher, put them both inside then spun on his heel to face her with a look of determination. 'You will be the most amazing mommy ever and I will be the most awesome, stylish uncle that any little poppet ever had. Ooh, I wonder if the baby will have your stunning red hair? Here's hoping as I can see the tiny wardrobe already, hues of green and copper and, of course, yellow. Goodness, there're so many choices ahead of us...'

'What would I do without you?' Libby cut in.

'You'll never know 'cos I'm not going anywhere. This baby will be loved and cherished. And my adorable niece or nephew will have anything in life that he or she wants.'

Everything except a father, Libby thought, but said nothing as she swallowed the lump in her throat and blinked away the last of the tears stinging the corners of her eyes.

'And we will throw the best birthday parties ever!' Bradley continued, his face animated with excitement and his hands moving around wildly. 'I can see them now. Like tiny carnivals with rides and cotton candy and a petting zoo.'

Libby's lips began to curl upwards as her spirits lifted just a little. 'You're spoiling the baby and we still have seven months to meet him or her.'

'Of course it's my responsibility as Uncle Bradley. I'm in your baby's life for ever.'

Libby felt a stab in her heart, wishing the father of her baby would be in their lives for ever too, but that would never be. She had no clue where he had gone. The hospital could not give Libby a forwarding address and he had not mentioned leaving to anyone other than his short, and apparently sudden, resignation email.

Clearly, she meant nothing to him. Neither had their time together been as special as she had imagined. It had all been in her head. She had romanticised the entire affair. She feared he might feel the same about the child they had created but she would never know because there was no way for her to tell him.

As he sat staring out across the brilliant blue water Dr Daniel Dimosa's thoughts unexpectedly returned to the gorgeous redheaded nurse who, only months earlier, had unknowingly made him forget about the uncertainty of his future, if only for a few short weeks. She was sweet and kind and the woman he'd wanted but knew he couldn't have. Not for ever, at least.

Daniel had fought the attraction over the time they had spent together while he had been Acting Head of ER. He had valiantly attempted to keep their relationship professional. But he had failed. Her nursing skills, genuine empathy with patients and wonderfully warm, kind manner was nothing he had witnessed before. She would work past her shift to allay the fears of patients and their families, go the extra mile to transfer her knowledge to inexperienced medical students, and make all the medical team around her feel included and important. And against everything he had promised himself, he had begun to fear he was close to falling in love.

No matter how much he'd tried, Daniel couldn't ignore his feelings for her. He would look for excuses to spend time with her even over a coffee in the early hours of the morning at the twenty-four-hour cafeteria, but he'd still kept the conversation about their mutual love of medicine. Nothing about the past and nothing about the future.

He couldn't allow himself to make promises he couldn't keep. Daniel had known it was only a matter of time until he would need to leave. He had long known he could not in any good conscience promise a future to any woman and for that reason he had kept his love life to flings with women who wanted nothing more.

And for that reason Daniel had left that night without saying goodbye or offering an explanation. It wasn't his to offer. Instead, he had climbed from the warmth of the bed they had shared and disappeared into the night. He had left without waking the woman who was beginning to steal his heart. He thought back to the moment he had gently moved the strand of red hair resting on her forehead and tenderly kissed her one last time as she'd lain sleeping like an angel. His heart had ached with every step he'd taken away from her. Knowing he would never see her again. Never make love to her again. Never hold her again.

He knew it had been a mistake to take their relationship from that of colleagues to lovers but the passion had overtaken them and he had given in to his desire to have her in his arms, if only for one night.

Before he'd closed the door he'd silently mouthed, *I will never forget you, Libby.*

Then he had walked away, knowing there was no choice.

He had done it to protect her…and now he had to do everything he could to forget her. And he hoped she would do the same.

CHAPTER ONE

'I LOVE YOU, BILLY.'

'I luff you, Mommy.'

'You need to be a very good boy for Grandma while I'm gone,' Libby said, blinking back tears as she squatted down to the little boy's eye level and ran her fingers through his thick black hair. 'I'll only be away for a few days, and I'll miss you very much.'

'I'll be good. I promith,' he said, and threw his little arms around her neck.

'Grandpa's waiting in the car to take me to the airport. I need to go now but I'll be back soon.'

'Grandma told me seven sleeps.'

'That's right,' Libby replied, then kissed his chubby cheek. 'I love you to the moon and back.'

'I luff you this much,' he said, stretching his arms as far as he could.

Libby stood up, ruffled his hair gently

and redirected her attention to her mother. 'Please call me if you need me, anytime, day or night. My cell phone will always be on. I'll call every night but if Billy gets a sniffle or a tummy ache or just needs to talk to me during the day or night, please call me.'

'I will, I promise. Billy will be fine with us. Now go or you'll miss your plane,' her mother told her as they all walked to the car, which was idling in the driveway with her father at the wheel and her luggage already in the trunk. Libby climbed into the front passenger seat and as the car drove away she watched her son holding his grandmother's hand and waving goodbye. She felt empty already and the car hadn't left the street.

'Now, don't you go worrying while you're away, poppet,' her father said as they merged into the freeway traffic. 'We'll take good care of our grandson.'

'I know you will, Dad,' she said, trying to blink away the tears threatening to spill onto her cheeks. 'It's just I've never been away from Billy and it's…it's…'

'I know it's hard, Libby, but, believe me, it's probably going to be a lot tougher on you than him. Worrying and missing your child is all part of being a parent,' he said with a wink and a brief nod in Libby's direction. 'But we'll keep him busy and your mother has an itinerary to rival a royal visit. I swear you get your organisational skills from her. We're off to the zoo tomorrow and the play-ground the next day, and on Thursday Brad-ley's heading over to take him out for ice cream and a walk on the beach, and he's got a play date with the neighbours' grandchil-dren on Saturday... Oh, I almost missed out a day. Your mother booked tickets for that new animated car movie at the cinema on Friday. I tell you we will all sleep well this week from sheer exhaustion.'

Libby McDonald listened to all her father was saying. She appreciated everything her parents had planned for Billy so much but it didn't help as her heart was being torn a little with each mile they travelled. She was thirty-three years of age, mother of the world's most adorable little three-year-old boy, single by choice, and she loved her son more than life itself and didn't want to be away from him.

'You might have fun in the Caribbean. It's not every day you get asked to fly to the other side of the country to tend to a wealthy pa-tient for a week on a luxury yacht. What was his name again?'

'Sir Walter Lansbury,' Libby replied as she looked out of the car window, feeling no excitement at the prospect.

'That's right.' Her father nodded as he flicked the indicator to change lanes. 'He's quite a philanthropist and a generous benefactor to the Northern Bay General Hospital. Even had a wing named after him, your mother told me.'

'Yes, he's very generous and that's why the hospital board agreed to his request to have me as his post-operative nurse while he cruises through the Caribbean for seven days and nights. It's quite ridiculous really. He should be at home, recovering, at seventy-nine years of age, not gallivanting on the open seas five weeks after a triple coronary artery bypass graft.'

'Sounds like he's a bit of an adventurer.'

'Or a risk-taker and a little silly.'

'A risk taker without doubt,' her father remarked. 'But he wouldn't have amassed a fortune if he was silly.'

Libby didn't answer because she was completely averse to risk-taking and Sir Walter taking one with his health made him silly in her opinion. She had taken a risk falling in love and that had all but ensured she would never take another unnecessary risk.

She planned everything about her life and she liked it that way. Libby McDonald hated surprises and risks in equal amounts. Her life was settled and organised and was almost perfect, except for the occasional night when she couldn't fall asleep and her thoughts turned to Billy's father. But they were becoming fewer and fewer and she hoped in time she would all but forget him.

'We never know what the universe has in store for us. This trip might be a life-changing experience for you,' her father continued as he checked his rear-view mirror and took the next exit from the freeway. 'All I do know is that Sir Walter has secured himself the finest cardiac nurse in the whole country.'

Libby smiled at her father's compliment but she was far from convinced he was right. She felt certain there had to be other nurses who would jump at the opportunity but the hospital board had insisted she go. And there was no get-out-of-jail-free card attached to an order from the board. It was signed and sealed and in less than a week she had been packed and on her way to nurse the generous benefactor she had cared for after his heart surgery. How she wished at that moment that she had been in ER and not in his recovery team.

* * *

Later that day, Libby's flight finally landed in Miami and she caught a cab to the Four Seasons Hotel where a room had been booked for her by Sir Walter's assistant. Being a few hours ahead of the west coast it was getting late in Miami and the sun had set so she ordered room service, called home and said goodnight to Billy and, after eating dinner, she ran a hot bath. Surprisingly she had managed to doze just a little on the five-hour flight. Business class, courtesy of her temporary employer, was as luxurious as she had heard. But with no sleep the night before as she'd tossed about in her bed at home, she was close to exhaustion when she finally climbed into her king-size hotel bed and drifted off to sleep.

The next morning Libby woke, went for a brisk walk before she ate breakfast in her room, checked out of the hotel, and caught a cab to the marina. She was due there at eleven. Her stomach began to churn as the cab drew closer. The previous day's uneasy feeling was returning and while it was in its infancy, she feared it could gain momentum quickly.

She lowered her oversized sunglasses and

looked through the cab window at the busy road leading to the wharf and prayed that the week would pass quickly and there would be no surprises. None at all. Pushing her glasses back up the bridge of her nose, Libby collapsed back into the seat, second-guessing herself.

Suddenly her thoughts began to overwhelm her. The sensible, well-organised life she had created felt a little upside down and it weighed heavily on her. Her throat suddenly became a little dry and her palms a little clammy. The air-conditioner in the car suddenly didn't seem enough and she wished she hadn't agreed to the week-long assignment on the open seas.

She knew she would miss Billy terribly. He was her world and her reason for getting up each day, the reason she kept going, determined to create a life for the two of them.

Suddenly her cab driver made a U-turn and her hand luggage fell onto her lap and she heard a thud as her suitcase toppled over in the trunk. She rolled her eyes, quite certain that Bradley had packed more than she would need. But she hadn't argued as she'd had no idea what she would need. She had no clue since she had never done anything like it before.

Libby McDonald had been playing it safe, very safe, and now she felt at risk of becoming a little…lost at sea.

'We're about two minutes away, miss,' the driver said. 'I'm taking a shortcut through the back streets as the traffic jam ahead would make it fifteen.'

'Thank you,' she said, smiling back at him in the rear-view mirror. His voice had brought her back to the present. It was not the time or the place for doubting herself. She had to quash her rising doubts because there was no turning back.

The cab was weaving around a few narrow streets until finally Libby could see the ocean and rows of yachts of all shapes and sizes.

'I think this is your stop,' he announced, finally coming to a halt.

Once again, she dropped her glasses to rest on the bridge of her nose and, in an almost teenage manner, peered out of the cab window again. She spied the yacht—gleaming, magnificent and standing tall and pristine in the perfectly still blue water. It was the most magnificent ship she had ever seen. Not that she'd seen any up close and personal. Her experience was from travel shows on cable television but she had not expected it to be so grand and beautiful in reality. Regal was the word that came to mind as her gaze roamed the structure and her eyes fell on the name emblazoned across the bow, *Coral Contessa*. That was definitely the one. She had been told that Sir Walter Lansbury had named it after his beloved late wife, Lady Contessa.

Libby's stomach knotted with trepidation. The yacht was going to be both her workplace and temporary home for the next seven days. Suddenly motion sickness, or something like it, came over her even though she was still on dry land.

While she had worked in both Emergency and Cardiology at the hospital for over seven years, she knew nothing of nursing on a ship. And that bothered her. Libby had consulted with the cardiologist a few days before she'd left for her trip and had been reminded that their patient had had a post-operative elevated blood pressure and a BMI that indicated he needed to lose at least twenty pounds. To the frustration of his specialist, Sir Walter loved bad food, cigars and strong liquor and he didn't take his health as seriously as he did the stock market.

Initially, Libby had also been concerned about the number of passengers and crew and whether she would be responsible for everyone, and how many that would be in total.

She had been reassured by the hospital that there would be no more than twelve to fourteen other passengers and eleven crew members, including the two-person medical team. They felt confident most of the passengers would come on board in good health and remain that way for the duration of the cruise.

She would be focused on her client and occasionally managing passengers' nausea, the effects of too much sun or too much alcohol, the odd strained muscle or twisted ankle. There was always the risk of more serious conditions but Libby hoped her cruise on the *Coral Contessa* would be uneventful, busy enough to keep her mind occupied but not overwhelming. Nothing would go wrong, she reminded herself, if the number one patient followed their advice.

Everyone agreed Sir Walter would be better off not going to sea five weeks after heart surgery and instead resting at home but, being headstrong, he clearly wasn't accepting that. She hoped the ship's doctor was equally headstrong and together they could manage their patient.

Libby wasn't entirely sure if the impetus for her decision to accept the job offer had been Bradley's contagious excitement or another one of her parents' well-meaning heart-to-heart talks about her taking chances and moving on with her life.

She was still young, they constantly reminded her, and she had so much to experience and a whole world to see. And Billy needed to grow up knowing she was not only the best mother he could wish for but also a strong independent woman who had a career and a life. Just thinking about him, her fingers reached for the antique locket hanging on a fine silver chain around her neck and she held it in the warmth of her palm. Inside was a photograph of the beautiful dark-haired, blue-eyed boy. He was the image of the father he would never know.

Libby stilled her nerves and blinked away the unexpected threat of tears she was feeling at the thought of being away from her little boy. It was only a week at sea, she reminded herself firmly, and her parents wanted so much to spend quality time with their beloved grandson. But she and Billy had never been apart for more than a day in three years. He was the light in her life and she wasn't sure how she would cope.

True to his word, Bradley had thrown a birthday party for Billy every year and had hosted his third birthday two days before

Libby had left. Their family and friends had come and showered Billy with presents as they always did, and those with small children had brought them along to enjoy the celebrations, including a face painter. Bradley had enthusiastically dressed as a giant sailor bear. He thought he'd looked like a furry member of the Village People—Libby wasn't sure but the image still made her smile.

There had been way too much cake, far too many sweets and more balloons than Libby had ever seen, courtesy of her mother. Everyone had had a wonderful day but Libby had been preoccupied at times throughout the afternoon with doubts about her impending trip, although it had been pointless to fight the inevitable. The trip was going to happen. And everyone except Libby seemed very happy about that fact.

That night Bradley had insisted on helping her pack. He'd included a swimsuit and a light denim playsuit and a stunning silk dress that skimmed her ankles. It was deep emerald-green silk with a plunging neckline and nothing close to the practical clothes she generally wore, a going-away present from Bradley.

'Take a risk for once!' Bradley had told her

when she'd unwrapped his parting gift. 'You have the body for it, so flaunt it!'

Libby had frowned at him.

'It's perfect for you and what's the point in having a stylish BFF if you don't listen to me? Besides, it matches your gorgeous eyes so you have to take it.'

Libby had laughed and given Bradley a big hug. At six feet four he was almost a foot taller than her and she always felt secure in his hug, if not always secure in his choice of clothes for her. The outfit was very far removed from her usual conservative style. She wasn't sure she would wear it, because even if she was brave enough, she felt quite sure she wouldn't have the occasion to do so, but Bradley had insisted. He had released his arms from around her tiny waist, ignored her concerns, packed all of his choices in her luggage and had returned to her closet to find some sandals to complete the look.

'Let's face it, *all* of your cute outfits and shoes have been Christmas and birthday gifts from me,' he had said, with a pair of unworn gold high heels he had given her for Christmas the year before balanced in one hand while he pulled another dress from a hanger, along with a sarong and a wide-brimmed straw hat. He placed all of it neatly into her open suitcase. 'Anything conservative is staying home. I refuse to let my absolute best friend in the world morph into a soccer mom. You're too young for that. At least wait until Billy's actually old enough to play soccer.'

Libby smiled as she remembered his remark and silently admitted that what he'd said wasn't too far from the truth. She knew she would never wear most of the outfits Bradley had packed but she didn't argue. There would apparently be two ports of call, which meant that if Sir Walter wanted to go ashore she would visit the islands with him, and if not she would remain on board.

Bradley had done his research and had told her that golden sandy beaches, translucent underwater caves and exclusive private isles were awaiting her. He told her to go ashore whenever she had the chance and not to be a party pooper by staying in her cabin. As he'd held up the travel brochures, he'd insisted she should do everything she could. Clearly, he was going to live the next week vicariously through her.

Libby wasn't fussed about any of it and, to be honest, wanted to get the trip over and done with so she could get back to her real life, but she didn't tell him that. He was excited for her so she let him tell her all about the sightseeing. At least one of them was excited.

Together they'd continued to pack and had selected shorts, T-shirts, jeans, lightweight jackets and a summer dress that Libby thought were far more her style. It became a compromise, with Bradley less than enthusiastic about some of Libby's clothing choices but agreeing if it didn't mean his choices were sacrificed to make room for them. At the end of the packing, she'd looked at her bursting luggage, convinced it would be way too much since she was working on the ship not socialising, but again Bradley had insisted.

Through social media, he had found out that the luxury, multi-million-dollar yacht had a pool, an intimate movie theatre and even a rock-climbing wall, and he reminded her that while Billy would be well taken care of by his doting grandparents and his fabulous fashionista Uncle Bradley, she needed to have some fun.

'She's a beauty,' the cab driver told her, breaking into Libby's reverie as he climbed from the cab and popped the trunk.

'Yes, she is,' Libby agreed, as she collected her belongings from the back seat and met him at the rear of the car.

'I'm sorry I'm a bit awkward with bags,' he began as he reached into the trunk. 'My fingers are a bit twisted. I think it might be arthritis.'

Libby looked down at the hands of the driver as he took hold of her bag. 'May I take a look?' she asked softly.

'Sure, why not? Are you a doctor?'

'No, I'm a nurse,' she replied as she reached for his hands.

He held both hands quite still for Libby to examine. Immediately she could see quite clearly there was a thickening and tightening of tissue under the skin of both hands. It was affecting the ring and little fingers. Both fingers on the right hand were almost completely closed into his palm. She recognised the problem immediately.

'How long have you had this condition?'

'A few years now but it's been getting worse lately,' he told her with a voice that signalled acceptance of his fate. 'I'm worried if both hands close I might not be able to drive and that would make life tough for the family. I'm fifty-two years old and I'd like to drive for another ten years if I can. My daughter's getting married next year and she wants the big wedding with all the bells and whistles so I can't be out of work.'

Libby said nothing as she continued to examine his hands. 'I'm not an expert but you may have a condition called Dupuytren's contracture.'

'Is there a treatment for it?'

'If it is what I think, it can be managed,' she told him. 'And it's definitely worth your while seeing someone. You would need to be referred to a specialist. My father had the condition and that's why I'm aware of it.'

'My ma told me it was arthritis and there was no hope. It's in my genes, she told me. My pa had it, but he died nearly twenty years ago 'cos of his diabetes.'

'Again, I am not an expert but if you make an appointment with your regular doctor…'

"I haven't seen a doctor in over ten years,' he cut in. 'I've been healthy as an ox and haven't needed one.'

Libby was well aware that there was a genetic predisposition to the condition but Dupuytren's contracture could be aggravated by cirrhosis of the liver and the presence of certain other diseases, including diabetes, which she was now aware was in his family along with thyroid problems so a visit to the doctor was well overdue. It could uncover a hidden condition that needed to be managed. The man's hands might be a sign that something even more serious was happening out of sight.

'I would make a time and get a general check-up and blood work while you're there. We should all do that every year. I'm sure you want to be heathy and happy and dance with your daughter at her wedding.'

'I do,' he said. 'I'll make a time next week to see a doctor. Honest, I will.'

Libby smiled and paid the fare, including a generous gratuity, and then reached down for her belongings.

'Thank you for taking the time to talk to me. Not many people do that nowadays. Everyone's in a rush. It was real nice of you,' the driver continued as he slipped the cash into his shirt pocket. 'You're a princess and I think you're a real good nurse.'

Libby smiled again and then reached for the suitcase that he had managed to pull from the trunk and place on the kerb. 'You take care of yourself.'

'And you have a great trip. Hope you meet a prince on that yacht,' the man said before he climbed into the cab.

Libby suddenly felt a little flustered with the thought as she struggled to manage her belongings. She didn't want to meet a prince—

or any man for that matter. She just wanted to get the next week over and done with and return to the only man who mattered to her: her son. With a bag across her chest and a laptop case slipping from her shoulder, she reached for her large suitcase sitting on the pavement where the driver had placed it and tried to calm her nerves. It's only a week, she reminded herself. *Only a week*.

Accepting her fate, she drew in a deep breath, put a smile on her face and hoisted the slowly slipping laptop bag back up onto her shoulder and made her way to the walkway onto the yacht. The sun was shining down and she could feel the warmth through her thin T-shirt. As she climbed aboard, she could see the shining deck, perfectly arranged with black wicker outdoor seating, scattered with oversized striped cushions in striking colours. Everything about it was stunning, even the sky and sea matched perfectly.

Under different conditions she might have enjoyed herself. But Libby had a job to do and then get home. She had no intention of socialising. She had no intention of doing anything other than tending to the medical needs of Sir Walter.

Brushing away wisps of red hair that had

escaped her ponytail, Libby hoped that the days ahead would pass quickly.

Dr Daniel Dimosa stood at the bow of the *Coral Contessa*, looking out across the perfectly still blue water. His mood was reflective, borderline sombre. It was the first day of his final ocean placement, then it was time to return to his family. The time had come. He looked down at his phone and reread the last message from his mother.

My darling son,

Thank you so much for agreeing to return to your home and your rightful place.

Your father's condition has deteriorated further since the last time we spoke. He has not made any public appearances in the last week and he must abdicate very soon. There are days that he struggles to remember his advisors' names. Thankfully, he is still very aware of who I am, and my prayer is that our love for each other is strong enough to help us through the most difficult times ahead.

I know the people of Chezlovinka will be elated to see you take up your role as Crown Prince, just as your father and his father before him. Without you, my darling, I know there would be unrest and instability and I fear what may become of our land and the future of the people who so rely upon us.

Your loving mother xxxx

Daniel knew he had no choice but to stop running from his past and stop wondering what might have been. There were still question marks over the future, but he would deal with those in time. His own time. In his heart, he knew that he was destined to follow in his father's footsteps, perhaps in more ways than one. Early onset dementia was a genetic disease and he was not certain that it had eluded him.

He knew he would miss the spray of salt water on his face, the sounds of the gulls whenever they drew closer to shore, and the serenity of the endless blue horizon. And most of all the freedom to practise medicine. He drew a deep bitter-sweet breath of warm, humid air. Sadly, his love affairs with both the sea and medicine were drawing to an end at the same time.

Daniel knew he had to face the fact that his current way of life was over and no matter how much he wished it could be different, it couldn't. He was a realist. His path and his fate had been chosen the day he was born and now he had no choice but to return to his homeland. He had seven more days as Dr Daniel Dimosa before he turned his back on his life as a doctor and returned to his life as Crown Prince Daniel Edwardo Dimosa.

The breeze picked up and Daniel felt a familiar emptiness in his heart. He had grown accustomed to a life with no ties but it didn't stop him wishing for more and wanting to feel again how he had felt in San Francisco all those years ago. But he would never put a woman he cared so deeply for through what his mother had faced since his father's diagnosis five years earlier. The worry of not knowing when her husband and the man she had loved her entire life would look at her as if she was a stranger.

His expression fell further as he admitted to himself that this would be the last time he was on US soil for a very long time. It would make this trip even more poignant.

While the day was warm and calm at that moment, weather at sea was more unpredictable and prone to drastic change. Not unlike some of the women Daniel had bedded over the last four years while he'd been trying to forget the sweet, loving redhead who had so unexpectedly captured his heart. Wherever the ship docked there were women who were happy to share one night of pleasure with no strings attached. It was enjoyable, and both parties were happy to walk away knowing it would never be more than that. He forgot them as quickly as he met them and he felt sure they did the same.

A tic in Daniel's jaw began on cue, the way it always did when he thought back to the woman he had loved so briefly. With all of his being, he wished he had handled it differently or, better yet, never become involved. He wished he had been in a place where he could have explained everything and told her the truth but he hadn't been. He had been sworn to secrecy and he couldn't break that promise.

Daniel was a man of his word—both as a doctor and as Crown Prince Daniel Edwardo Dimosa.

Travelling had been all he had known for so long and he was reluctant to leave that way of life, but he was needed at home so his choices were limited. Daniel's father had carried the burden of royal responsibilities for a long time. Now, at only sixty years of age, his condition had worsened and Daniel would not turn his back on the man he both loved and admired and who was slowly being trapped inside his own deteriorating mind.

By taking over the throne, it would allow

his father to retain his dignity and see out his final days away from the scrutiny of the public eye. And keeping that secret was paramount to the economic security of the principality. There was really no debate. Daniel needed to be there for his father and for the small European principality of Chezlovinka.

Over the years there were times late at night when his thoughts sometimes wandered back to the woman he had left behind. He hoped she had forgotten him, married and had a family. She deserved that and more... even if it wasn't with him.

'Dr Dimosa,' the young concierge began, 'I thought I'd let you know the ship's nurse has just boarded and has headed to her cabin. You asked me to notify you.'

'Thank you,' Daniel replied, turning momentarily to acknowledge the young man then just as quickly turning back to the view.

His life was to be one of duty to the principality he was destined to rule. It would be a life without freedom.

And one without love.

CHAPTER TWO

LIBBY STOPPED OUTSIDE her allocated cabin and reached into her bag for the door swipe card she had been given by one of the three stewards. They had offered to take her bags to the cabin but she'd wanted a few moments alone to take in her surroundings, to be alone with her thoughts and steady her unsettled nerves.

She was huffing and puffing, as well as flustered and anxious again by the time she reached her cabin and felt quite silly having a bag large enough for a month-long vacation. What was she doing? Why hadn't she fought the board's decision? And why had she allowed Bradley to pack so many outfits into such a large suitcase?

Everything was suddenly a little overwhelming again.

She should be home with her son instead of on the other side of the country, and sailing even further away. It was like the other side of the world to Libby, and her world was her boy. She didn't want to be anywhere without him.

'Hello, there.'

Libby turned quickly to find a young woman with a mop of blonde curls and a wide smile approaching her.

'Oh, my goodness, it can't be,' the woman began, then took a step backwards and faltered momentarily. 'Libby McDonald? Is that you?'

Libby realised instantly that she knew the woman. Standing before her was one of her closest friends from junior high.

'Georgie? Georgie Longbottom? I can't believe it's you.'

Without hesitation, the two embraced with wide grins and genuine elation.

'How long has it been?' Libby began as she released her hold and stepped back a little. Her previous apprehension and nerves were temporarily replaced with a much-needed feeling of comfort and familiarity as their eyes scanned each other with their smiles still broad and their shared joy palpable. 'It must be…almost twelve years?'

'Thirteen actually. I remember because I returned to London at the end of my sophomore year. Our crazy fun year at Seaview

High was the best year of my school life,' Georgie confessed, then paused for a moment as a wistful smile washed over her pretty face. 'To be brutally honest, it was probably one of the best years my life, full stop. We were fancy free and had no idea just how tough the real world can be.'

Libby nodded, silently admitting the carefree days of the final years of senior school had been some of the best for her too. The reality of Georgie's words brought her back to reality. They were not seventeen, wide eyed and looking for an adventure any more. The Caribbean adventure that Libby was facing now was not one about which she was feeling any real level of excitement.

Life had certainly not turned out as Libby had expected…in so many ways. And it sounded as if life had not been perfect for Georgie either but Libby didn't want to dwell or complain or ask too many questions, at least not immediately, of the friend she had not seen in for ever. She wanted to live at least for a little while in the unexpected joy that seeing Georgie had brought to her.

'That was a wonderfully happy year, wasn't it?'

'Absolutely,' Georgie replied as she reached

for Libby's laptop bag that was slipping from her shoulder. 'What's your role on board?'

'Sir Walter's nurse. What about you, what brings you on board?'

'I'm Walter's chef again for this trip,' she replied. 'He's a lovely man and easy to work for. I've done the Caribbean trip a few times for him. I've also catered some of his large, exclusive parties in his UK residence. He has a place in Miami, another in San Fran and one in London, and I own a restaurant not far from his London home. He tells me often enough to boost my ego that my restaurant is his favourite in the world. Anyway, he invited me to have a working holiday in the Caribbean, overseeing the galley crew and making some fabulous desserts, and I couldn't say no.'

'That's so exciting and what a compliment. I never knew you wanted to be a chef,' Libby confessed. 'I never even knew you cooked.'

'It's a long story, but I found my passion in life after I left school. But enough about me. I want to hear all about your life and since your cabin is right next to mine, I'm sure we'll have lots of time to catch up. I saw your name on the room register half an hour ago. I knew you always wanted to be a nurse so I wondered if it could possibly be you, but I didn't want to get my hopes up because there's more than one Elizabeth McDonald in the world.'

'Yes, it's not an exotic or exciting name…'

'And you think Georgina Longbottom sounds like a rock star?'

Both girls laughed.

'Hey,' Georgie continued as she took Libby's laptop bag and put it on her own shoulder. 'Let's get you unpacked before the staff meeting.'

'I think I've over-packed.'

Georgie smiled again. 'I would have to agree with you on that…and from memory that's not like you. I was always the one with too many bags when we'd take off down the coast for a few days to one of those music festivals. You were always the sensible one with everything packed neatly into a backpack. Quite the minimalist. Clearly things have changed in regard to that.'

'My friend Bradley made me pack…'

'Bradley,' Georgia cut in, looking her friend in the eyes with a cheeky smile and her head tilted. 'Is he your other half?'

'No, Bradley's other half is Tom and he's super nice. I'll tell you all about him when we get inside, if I can fit all of this in the cabin.'

'We'll manage. The cabin's quite tiny but we can put the suitcase under the bunk.'

'Bunk?'

'Yes, bunk, but you have the cabin to yourself as there aren't too many staff on board so you have the choice of top or bottom bunk. It's not a stateroom like the guests have but it's quite nice in there.'

Libby smiled as she tried to recall the last time she had slept in a bunk. Then it came to her. 'Like at Big Bear camp?'

'Maybe a little, but this cabin has a porthole. It moves with the motion of the waves but you'll get used to it,' Georgie remarked with a half-grin.

Libby nodded as she retrieved her swipe card from the unlocked cabin door and they stepped inside. She was definitely older and she prayed wiser but the fact that she was on a luxury yacht so far from home had her doubting her wisdom. Seeing Georgie made her feel a lot better about the situation but it also brought back a time that had been uncomplicated and for the longest moment she wished she was that innocent again. A time when everything was exactly what it seemed. A time when she could trust people's intentions.

Libby drew a deep breath. 'I think the next seven days are going to be a lot better with you on board,' Libby said, feeling a little more relaxed than she had thirty minutes earlier.

'Have you been on many ships other than this one?' Libby asked, pushing unwanted thoughts of romance from her mind as she quickly checked out the cabin and found a small bathroom with a toilet, wash basin and shower. It was clean and compact like the rest of the accommodation and with Georgie's help she was quickly becoming more comfortable in her surroundings. She was gaining control in small ways and it was making her relax just a little.

'No, just Walter's. I'm busy running the restaurant so I can't afford the time to do it for anyone else.'

'You're back so I guess you must have enjoyed it.'

Georgie nodded. 'Yes, I did. It's stressful at times but so much fun and you end up becoming good friends with the other team members. Or even more sometimes.'

'Romance at sea. That sounds like a dreadful idea,' Libby said with a look of disdain. She couldn't think of anything worse at that moment.

'It's happened before and the doctor on this trip is ridiculously handsome—tall, dark and single—but he's too aloof for me. The crew all say he's a nice guy but he's way too mysterious. I'm over that type but maybe you…'

'Absolutely not. I'm definitely not looking for romance,' Libby cut in, shaking her head and feeling shivers run over her body. Tall, dark and mysterious was everything in a man she never wanted again.

'Never say never.'

'No, I can say never. Believe me, I'm not interested in anything other than looking after my patient, seeing some sights and then heading home to my…' Libby stopped, pulling herself up again from mentioning Billy. She decided to leave that conversation for later. She was already too emotional and she didn't want to talk about Billy and risk crying.

'Your…?'

'My…um…family. It's the first time I've been away in for ever.'

'Sometimes being thrown into new situations out of your comfort zone is the best way.'

'I'm not sure about that but I guess I'm going to find out.'

Daniel was waiting to meet the nurse who he had been told had boarded and was settling into her cabin. While there were still thirty minutes until the scheduled briefing with the captain, the rest of the ship's staff had already made their way to the deck. He wasn't sure why he was feeling anxious, but he couldn't ignore the stirring in the pit of his stomach. It was almost a feeling of déjà vu and it made him feel less than his usual relaxed self. There was more than enough time to prepare for the dozen or so passengers and their host and the *Coral Countess* would not be setting sail for another two hours, so there was nothing he could put his finger on at that moment, yet he was still uneasy.

The cabin that had been converted into a makeshift hospital room was next to Sir Walter's suite. With only five weeks since the long heart surgery, Daniel had requested it be set up to resemble as closely as possible a hospital room with everything he and the cardiac nurse would require should Sir Walter have any post-operative complications. It was uncommon but not impossible to suffer issues a few weeks post-op and he wished that Sir Walter had delayed the trip a little longer.

Daniel's sense of unease wasn't abating and he put it down to the fact that this would be his last voyage. He ran his fingers through his dark hair, took another deep breath and began pacing the pristine deck overlooking the helipad again, his mind slowly filling with remorse, regret and more than a little melancholy as he thought back over his life at sea and how it was coming to an end. At forty-one years of age, he had spent ten years of his medical career consulting in different hospitals all over the world and almost four tending to the needs of passengers on both private yachts and larger cruise liners. And twice he had tended to the needs of their families when one of the passengers had died at sea.

Daniel sighed as he thought back over the good, the bad and then the sad moments in both his personal and professional life. It had certainly been a mixed bag but he did not regret his decision to leave Chezlovinka and taste freedom for the last decade. He was also very grateful to his mother for encouraging and supporting his desire to pursue a medical career and now he would repay her by returning to rule so his father could abdicate.

Daniel lifted his chin defiantly at the thought of the life that lay ahead for him. There was so much he didn't know about his future. All that was certain and all that he could control was the next seven days on the *Coral Contessa*.

Georgie looked down at her watch. 'We'd best be off, then. We don't want to be late.'

'Late for what?' Libby asked, her blue eyes widening suddenly.

'Our briefing with the rest of the ship's crew, including our hunky mysterious medic. I mentioned it a moment ago.'

Libby shook her head and climbed to her feet. 'Of course, I'm sorry, you did mention it. I'm just a bit distracted.' Meeting the ship's doctor was not her focus. She was still worried about Billy and how he would cope without her. And how she would cope without him.

The last thing she wanted was to appear unprofessional in front of the rest of the crew so she was grateful that it was only Georgie in the cabin. She nervously brushed her jeans with her hands. There was no dust but it helped her to regain her composure.

'Hey, you'll be fine. Once we set sail you'll realise this is a piece of cake.'

'I hope so,' Libby replied, and quickly pulled a comb from her purse and hastily redid her ponytail, catching all the unkempt red wisps.

'If Dr Dimosa is easygoing underneath his moody Mediterranean demeanour, the trip will be a joy for you.'

Libby froze on the spot. Her stomach fell. 'Dr Dimosa is the ship's doctor?' she said, forcing the words past the lump that was forming in her throat. It was made of tears and anger and complete disbelief.

'Yes, Daniel Dimosa. He's the one I was talking about. Do you know him?'

Libby's pulse began to race and her stomach sank further. Dr Daniel Dimosa? *Her* Daniel? The man who had broken her heart and left without a word.

Billy's father.

Libby felt the colour drain from her face. Suddenly the cabin began to spin and she grabbed the edge of the desk to steady herself. An onslaught of emotions rushed at her as the blood drained from her head to feed her pounding heart. Libby felt herself falling and she was powerless to stop herself from crashing to the floor.

CHAPTER THREE

'WHAT EXACTLY HAPPENED before she fainted?' Daniel called down the corridor as he walked quickly with his medical bag in his hand. Concern was colouring his voice as he neared the cabin where Georgie was waiting outside. 'Was there a critical incident, or any sign she wasn't well?'

'No, nothing. I just told her that we needed to head to the deck for the captain's briefing with you.'

'How is she now?'

'She's conscious but on the floor still.' She motioned with her hand as she opened the cabin door but paused outside. 'I placed a pillow under her head and called for you. I asked her to remain where she was until you arrived. The fall was very sudden and it doesn't make sense…unless she has an underlying health issue that she never mentioned during our conversation.'

Daniel moved past Georgie, stepped inside and looked over to the young woman lying on the floor. He was forced to steady himself on the frame of the doorway. His whole world changed in an instant. Nurse Elizabeth McDonald was Libby McDonald. The woman he had loved and left. The same woman who had never completely left his thoughts.

And the woman he had never thought he would see again.

Daniel stared in silence, so many conflicting thoughts running through his mind. Over the years since they had parted he would sometimes be reminded of her by the sight of a woman with long red hair in the crowd or hearing a laugh like hers. And he would wonder what would have happened between them if only his life had been different.

But it wasn't different and now more than ever he knew that.

He stilled his nerves, crossed the small cabin like a man possessed, and knelt down beside her. While her breathing was laboured, she was conscious and staring at the ceiling. He fought an unexpected but strangely natural desire to pull her into his arms.

'Will she be okay?' Georgie asked, breaking into his thoughts.

He had to remind himself that he was the ship's doctor, nothing more, although being this close to Libby again was suddenly making him wonder how easy that would be.

Placing his fingers on her neck, he took her pulse. It was racing but strong. Her eyes were open and looking towards the ceiling. And they were the most brilliant green, just as he had remembered. She was alert but saying nothing. Her pupils, he could see, were equal in size and not dilated.

'Libby, it's me. Daniel.'

Libby closed her eyes and turned her face away from his as he spoke. She said nothing to even acknowledge his presence in the cabin.

He knew he deserved her reaction. 'I had no idea you were the nurse on this trip. I guess I never thought of you as Elizabeth.'

Still nothing.

'I've always thought of you as Libby.'

She slowly turned back to face him. He saw her eyes were as cold as ice, her lips a hard line on her beautiful face. 'I don't care how you thought of me,' she said coldly, before she rolled her face away from his again, and he watched as she wiped at a tear with the back of her hand. 'Just leave, Daniel. I don't need you here.'

'I'm not going anywhere,' Daniel said before he turned to Georgie. 'Please leave us alone. I can take it from here.'

From Georgie's expression he could see she was clearly perplexed but she did as he asked and walked from the cabin, pulling the cabin door closed behind her.

Using her elbows as support, Libby tried to ease herself into an upright position.

'Please don't move,' he told her, and placed his warm hand gently on her wrist.

'Don't…don't touch me,' she said, pulling her arm free. 'I need to leave, now.'

'I'm checking your vitals before you're going anywhere.'

'Take them if you must,' she said curtly. 'Give me a clean bill of health then I'm leaving the ship. There's no way on God's earth I'm spending the next seven days working with you.'

'Let's deal with that in a minute. First you have to remain still while I check your BP.' Swiftly and efficiently, Daniel removed the blood pressure cuff from his medical bag and wrapped it around the arm she had reluctantly given him. The result took only a few moments. 'Ninety-eight over fifty.'

'I have low blood pressure,' she spat back as she quickly unwrapped the pressure cuff and shoved it in Daniel's direction. 'It's nothing out of the normal range for me. I'm fine.'

Daniel looked at the cuff lying in his hands and then back at Libby. There was so much he wanted to say but couldn't. And things he was feeling that scared his cold heart.

He had to stay focused and ignore his reaction to the woman who was so close to him he could smell the perfume resting delicately on her skin. What they had shared was in the past and had to remain there, he reminded himself. He had left her bed in the early hours of that morning for good reason.

Nothing had changed. In seven days he would leave the yacht and begin to transition to ruling the principality; he wasn't about to risk the distance he had purposefully put between Libby and himself when he had walked away.

It was not just about two people any more. He had to think of his father and the people of Chezlovinka.

'I understand why you're reacting the way you are,' he began, his voice low and controlled. 'It's justified and I deserve it but it was a long time ago.'

'You think you understand? Really? I don't think you could possibly understand,' she said in an almost breathless voice as she glared at him again.

'I understand more than you'll ever believe.' He was fighting his mind's desire to remember back to the wonderful weeks they shared and their last night together.

'I doubt it because if you truly did, then you wouldn't have left San Francisco without the decency of an explanation. It's been four years, Daniel. That's more than enough time to reach out.'

'I couldn't, Libby. It's complicated.' He moved back, creating distance between them. Distance she clearly wanted and he definitely needed.

'Complicated? That's the best you can come up with after all this time?' she responded, shaking her head. 'That's beyond pathetic but I don't care any more.'

'I don't know what else to say,' he began, knowing that she wanted and deserved more but he was not ever going to be in a position to let her know the truth.

'Don't bother trying, Daniel. There's nothing you could say that would make a scrap of difference now. It could have once, but that was a very long time ago.'

Daniel took a deep breath. 'As I said, I had my reasons…'

Libby looked away, staring at nothing. 'We all have choices in life. You're just not telling me the reason why you made yours.'

Daniel chose to say nothing because there was nothing he could say. He couldn't admit that he had never meant to take their relationship as far as making love to her that night because he had not been free to become involved. He could not tell her about his family, his destiny to rule the principality, or the secret they were all forced to hide from the world to maintain the stability of the small principality. His hands were tied.

'Honestly, Daniel, I don't give a damn.' Libby's voice was cold and matter-of-fact. 'But you can do the right thing now by getting out of my way and letting me off this ship. Find yourself a new nurse and give my sincere apologies to Sir Walter.'

Daniel shook his head. 'I wish it was that simple but it's not. Unfortunately, you can't leave the yacht, Libby.'

'Just watch me.'

'No matter how angry you are with me, you can't just leave,' he replied as he ran his fingers through the black waves of his hair. 'I need to have a qualified cardiac nurse to assist with his care.'

'Are you serious? I'm expected to care what you need?'

'No, but you need to consider what Walter needs, and that's an experienced nurse. He's five weeks post-operative. I can't have just anyone on board.'

'Then get an experienced temp from an agency,' she cut in angrily. 'I'm not that special.'

Daniel disagreed silently. Libby was very special in many ways but he would never be able to tell her that. 'It can't happen, Libby. I'm sorry. It's just not possible.'

No matter how many nights he had ached to have her lying in his arms, to feel the warmth of her body next to his and taste the sweetness of her kiss again, Daniel knew now more than ever he had to keep her at arm's length. He had to keep their relationship the way it had begun all those years ago before he'd overstepped the mark.

'I need to have a competent nurse with your experience and qualifications,' he told her, quickly re-establishing the professionalism that was required.

Libby stared at him for a moment, her eyes roaming every inch of his face before turning her gaze back to the ceiling. Daniel felt even more confused. While she had every right to be angry and distant, it was as if there was something more behind her words. He wasn't sure if it was just more anger but there was something. Something she was holding back from saying.

'I'm sure there's a nurse who can fit the bill,' she said in a voice devoid of emotion.

'We need clearances and we're leaving in less than two hours. The process can't happen that quickly.'

'Call someone. Expedite it. I'm sure Sir Walter is well connected.'

Daniel shook his head. 'No one is that well connected, not even Walter. There's a process that can't be fast-tracked when you're sailing in international waters and that's removing the most obvious and pressing fact that we have a patient with specific needs. Walter's condition is precarious. He needs a highly skilled nurse and you agreed to travel with him. You have a duty of care and you signed a contract.'

'The board at the Northern Bay General Hospital signed that agreement...'

'On your behalf and, again, for good reason, they have put their reputations on the line. Walter is one of America's wealthiest men and I imagine he's also a very generous benefactor to the hospital. He's also in need of high-quality, specialised care. For all of these reasons, you have to stay on board. I'm sorry, Libby, there's really no option. The ship can't set sail without you and I don't think you want to have Walter and the board suing you for breach of contract.'

Libby slowly got to her feet as Daniel rose to his with his hand extended to her. She ignored his offer of assistance and used the bunk to steady herself.

'Then write me a sickness certificate and clear me to leave so they can't sue me. Tell them I have an unexpected medical condition.'

'But you don't have any condition, Libby. I can't lie.'

He watched as she took a deep breath and considered his words. Again, her demeanour was so different from that of the woman he had met all those years before; the hurt clearly still ran deep but there was something else. There was something less carefree about her. Something behind those beautiful eyes that he couldn't quite work out.

'You lied to me…'

'I didn't lie, Libby. I left without an explanation. I never lied.'

'Well, if you find that acceptable, how about I do the same now? I'll just leave without an explanation, if you believe that's acceptable behaviour,' she said in a controlled but clearly hostile voice. 'I deserve the right to walk away just like you did. The only difference is that you'll know why...and it's your choice whether to tell them or not.'

Daniel nodded, accepting the truth in her words. 'I deserve that.'

'Yes, you do and I deserve your help to get me off this yacht now.' She closed her eyes and shook her head.

Daniel wished he could help her but he couldn't. 'If I could I would but—'

'Write the certificate and I'll be gone. It won't matter if Walter delays setting sail for one day. They can all stay aboard here in the port and party into the early hours.'

'Unfortunately, even a delay of two hours let alone a day to secure a new nurse would cause Walter to miss his niece Sophia's engagement party.'

'Engagement party? What engagement party?' she demanded as she slumped back down on the lower bunk shaking her head. 'I thought this was just a week's cruise.'

'It is, with a small engagement party in San Lucia. He's brought his favourite chef from London to oversee the catering. Guests are coming in from all over the world to meet him there.'

'So, that's it, then. It's a fait accompli. I'm forced to stay.'

'I'm sorry, Libby.' Daniel's long fingers rested on his clenched jaw as he looked at the woman over whom he had lost countless nights of sleep—from both guilt and the realisation that he would never find a woman like her again.

Her face held a mix of anger and hopelessness. 'Trapped on this ship and expected to work with you? It's so unfair and you know it.'

'It is unfair, but I will find a compromise. I will make our working time together minimal. We can visit Walter at separate times and any incidents with the other passengers we will handle the same way unless there's an emergency...' he began, just as he received a pager alert. He looked down momentarily at his device, then moved towards the door. 'If you agree to those terms we can work this out for the next week.'

Libby chewed the inside of her cheek anxiously. For her there was more to think about than just not wanting to spend any time with Daniel. There was Billy to consider. Daniel had no idea he was father to her son. How would he react to knowing that? Would he even believe Billy was his child? And if he did believe her, would he actually care? It was a dilemma she'd never thought she would have to face. She tried to calm her breathing as Daniel left, closing the door behind him. She was stuck between a rock and a hard place and there was no choice but to agree to Daniel's terms. Being sued was not an option. She had lost her heart once to the man— and almost her mind—when he'd left, and she wasn't about to lose her home and her future because of him.

There was so much at risk by staying but even more by leaving. For nearly four years she had resigned herself to never seeing Daniel again, never having to think about telling him that he had a son. And now she was going to be at sea for seven days and seven nights with the father of her child. The father of the little boy who was so much like him. The deep blue eyes that looked up at her every night when she tucked him into bed were his father's eyes. The black hair that she smoothed with her hands in the morning when Billy ran to her, arms outstretched, for a cuddle was his father's hair. The skin that turned a beautiful golden hue in the summer sun, that too was his father's Mediterranean skin.

But when Daniel had disappeared, Libby had had neither the money nor the desire to hire someone to find him. To tell him that he had a son he might not even have wanted.

But now it was an option. Now there was the opportunity to tell him and she was confused, *terribly* confused about how he would react to the news. The man she had fallen in love with and who she had invited into her bed would care, but the man who had walked away might not care at all and that would break her heart all over again.

Libby watched as the door slowly opened again. Her heart picked up speed and she felt it pumping erratically. She dropped her gaze as Daniel stepped back inside the cabin. She didn't want to look at him. She was worried she would see her precious son in his eyes and consequently soften towards Daniel. She needed time to think. Time to work out in her mind what was best for her son. Not for her and not for Daniel. Her thoughts were only on what was best for Billy. He was the innocent one and needed to be considered above anyone else. Did she have the right to hide Daniel's son from him? Did his behaviour, leaving without an explanation or a forwarding address, take away his right to know he was a father? But if she told him, and he became a part of his son's life in some capacity, could he leave again without warning and the next time break Billy's heart?

She needed time and a clear head to sort it out. She wasn't going to rush into making a life-changing decision for Billy.

Libby wondered if time on the yacht would allow her to learn more about Daniel, get to know the real man and try her very best not to let their failed relationship influence her decision. Libby knew she had to make a truly informed choice, not just react emotionally. Perhaps that was what fate had planned—time for her to learn as much as she could about Daniel and allow her to make the very best choice for Billy.

'Your decision?'

Libby continued looking down at the cabin floor as she shifted her feet nervously. Little did he know that she had two decisions to make...

'Let's be honest, Daniel, I don't really have much of a choice. It's been made for me. I have to stay.'

'Thank you, Libby. It's best for everyone.'

'We'll see,' she told him. Her heart was still beating out of her chest. She had so much at risk. There was much to protect and consider for the next week.

'There's one more thing,' he said as he turned to leave. 'I'm sorry, Libby, but you'll still have to attend the briefing with the senior members of the crew on the stern deck in thirty minutes. It's a regulation procedure. After that I will do my best to ensure there's minimal contact between us.'

Libby nodded. She was still struggling to process it all.

'Fine, but I want minimal contact, Daniel. I don't care how you arrange that but you need to make it happen,' she said, her words short and her tone curt. 'And don't even try to change the terms of this arrangement. If you do, I swear I'm getting off this ship at the first port and you'll be the one explaining why.'

CHAPTER FOUR

'ARE YOU OKAY, LIBBY?' Georgie asked as she stepped back inside the cabin, her big brown eyes even larger than before. 'I was so shocked when you fainted.'

'I'm okay. I think I was just overwhelmed. Maybe I didn't drink enough water and my blood pressure fell.'

Georgie's expression changed and Libby watched as her old friend closed the cabin door slowly, and purposefully moved closer as if she was about to learn a secret that could bring down a nation. 'Libby, from the day we met all those years ago at school we connected and we could never hide anything from each other. Nothing's changed; it's like we were sisters in a previous life.'

'I know but…' Libby began, then stopped, knowing she couldn't lie to her friend.

'Is there something you want to share with me? The way he looked at you, and the way he spoke, it was more than a little bit obvious you two have chemistry and if it's old chemistry, then it just re-ignited in this cabin.'

'It's nothing.' Libby stiffened at the question and felt her pulse pick up again. But nothing had re-ignited, she reminded herself. It was just the shock of seeing him and the decisions that came with having him so close to her.

'Oh, really, nothing? One, he called you Libby and, two, he said, "It's me, Daniel." And if that wasn't enough, he asked me to leave the cabin. Why would he do that unless he wanted to have a private conversation with you? You two definitely have history. You can tell me to butt out but I know there's something there.'

Libby couldn't talk her way out of it. She respected Georgie too much. She had no choice but to tell her part of the story. Just not everything.

'We dated briefly, *very* briefly a few years back. It feels like a lifetime ago.'

'I knew it,' Georgie said crossing the room and sitting on the bed beside her friend. 'However brief, and however it ended, it's clear to me that it was rather an intense relationship. It's so obvious that it wasn't just a casual fling for either of you.'

Libby closed her eyes and drew a deep breath. Once again, she was feeling overwhelmed with the reality of it all. Georgie's questions, while well intentioned, were confrontational and almost too much to handle. 'It's complicated.'

'I'm sorry, Libby, I didn't mean to pry. You don't have to go into it. I overstepped good manners and I do apologise, truly. I mean, by the look of you now and the expression on his face, what you shared might be better left alone, at least for now.'

'I'm sorry, Georgie. I'm not up to talking about it. Maybe later.'

'Absolutely. Whenever you're ready,' she replied as she reached out and embraced Libby. 'Like they say in the Hollywood movies, "I have your back, girl."'

With the kindness of Georgie's embrace, Libby found a ray of hope amongst the rubble that had suddenly become her life. Trapped at sea with Billy's father, the man whom she had loved deeply but briefly, was a disaster she had not seen coming. 'Thank you.'

Georgie finally released her hold. 'Men... can't live with them and apparently you can't sail without them.'

Libby nodded. She was still on very shaky ground with her emotions but somehow she had to dig down and find the strength to get through the cruise and make what could be the single most important decision in her life. And in her son's life. Her stomach was churning as she battled with doubts about making the right decision for everyone. And her own feelings about Daniel. Were they truly dead and buried?

'I guess if I have to go to the briefing, I might as well get it over and done with,' she announced, getting to her feet and lifting her chin and making her way to the cabin door, her heart pounding with every step.

Moments later, Libby and Georgie arrived on the deck where they found the rest of the crew waiting. Libby looked around her but didn't take in too much. It was by far the biggest yacht at the dock—and the most luxurious—but Libby was oblivious to all of it. Nothing was registering with her. Her mind was racing in many directions, all of them leading back to Daniel.

'Hello, there, I'm Captain Mortimer but you can call me Eric.' The captain acknowledged Libby and Georgie's arrival with a smile. He was a man in his late fifties, not particularly tall, with a kind face and short hair just beginning to grey at the temples. He was dressed in a white uniform, complete with epaulettes and a captain's cap, all with the *Coral Contessa* insignia.

Sir Walter really did like a very professional-looking crew; the younger, blond and slightly taller man next to Captain Mortimer wore the same uniform. There was nothing casual about this yacht. 'I have the pleasure of navigating this magnificent vessel for the next eight days and with any luck this weather will hold up and it will be quite lovely. We'll be setting sail this afternoon and cruising out across the Caribbean Sea for the next three days.

'On day four we'll be docking at Martinique. You can work out between yourselves who'd like to go ashore that day. We'll anchor there for about six hours to allow the guests to tour the island. At seventeen hundred hours we'll once again set sail with the intention of docking the next day around eleven-hundred hours in San Lucia.

'On this second and final stop we will remain in port for the day and the night so those who missed leave on Martinique can take some time in San Lucia. On the sixth day we hoist anchor at zero six hundred hours for the trip back across the Caribbean Sea to Miami. Any questions?'

Libby heard every word from the captain

but didn't retain too much as she was distracted by Daniel's presence so close to her after so many years. It was like a nightmare and one she wished she could wake from to find herself in her bed, in her home, hearing the giggles of her son playing in his room.

She blinked, hoping to make this reality disappear, but it didn't. She tried not to look in Daniel's direction but was powerless to prevent herself. She was drawn to him like a moth to a flame that would undoubtedly burn her if she got too close. He cut a powerful silhouette dressed in the starched white uniform too, a stark contrast to the darkness of his tanned skin. She watched as he stood alone, resting his lean fingers on the railing and staring out to sea. His look was far away but he didn't appear cold or arrogant. She couldn't help but notice he looked like a man in pain.

She didn't want to stare at him; she wanted to be able to look away; she wanted to hate him—and part of her did, but there was something in his expression that confused her. The pain in his eyes looked real. It was coming from somewhere deep inside and for some inexplicable reason Libby suddenly cared. Her reaction didn't make sense.

She should have been happy to see him

looking sad but she wasn't. She was seeing a man who looked like he was at war with himself. The cleft in his jaw was just as she remembered it. The blackness of his hair falling in soft waves, like the ocean, had not changed. In fact, everything about him was just the way she remembered, except for the almost overwhelming sadness. That was new. And somewhat perplexing for her.

For the first time in a long while Daniel was unsure how to behave, how to manage the situation and his own feelings. So he chose to remain silent and look out to sea. Look towards where they would be travelling for the next week and wish it to be over. He couldn't change the outcome so every moment would be difficult for him as he now knew it would be for Libby too. She had every right to be angry with him. His behaviour, without explanation, had been appalling. And he couldn't provide any explanation.

While he had imagined his last assignment at sea would be challenging, he could never had dreamt just how much.

He did not want to make it obvious to anyone else that he and Libby had once been as close as two people could ever be so he would make all communication minimal. Theirs had been a love affair that should never have happened. But he still wished with all his heart that it had never had to end.

'Let's go around the group and introduce ourselves and since we'll be working and living closely together for the next week perhaps tell us something interesting about you,' Captain Mortimer began, bringing Daniel back to the task at hand. Meeting everyone. 'Well, you know me so let's begin with our First Mate, Steve.'

'Thanks Eric, I'll keep it brief since I don't want to bore you all with stories of my perfect childhood, college sporting prowess or my new golden retrievers. I'm Steve Waterford. I've been First Mate for about five years now, and it's my second stint on the *Coral Contessa*. I was raised in Boston and still live there with said dogs when I'm not at sea. Boris is six months old and Molly's three months old and into everything, including my boxers drawer.' Steve smiled and then looked towards the casually attired man at his left, who was rolling his eyes but smiling. His head was clean shaven and he had a beard and wore heavy black glasses.

'Probably too much information, Steve. I'm Laurence Mitchell and I'm the Chief Engineer and I've been working on various yachts and cruise ships for just over six years. I've worked three stints with Eric and Steve. I'm a native New Yorker and also still live there when I'm not on the high seas.'

'I'm Stacey Langridge, the *Contessa's* purser,' the tall blonde woman began. She too was in uniform. 'This is my second cruise with Eric and I think I've worked with Steve more times than I can remember but I'm new to this ship. I grew up in SoCal near Venice Beach but now I live in Miami. I made the move over here about a year ago with my husband. No dogs in my life…although I've dated a few over the years.' She laughed then followed suit and looked to her left.

'I'm Daniel Dimosa, I'm half of the medical team.' Daniel kept his words brief. He had no desire to socialise or to mention anything about his personal life so he looked over in Georgie's direction, willing her to step up next.

'Georgie Longbottom. I'm from the UK, although I'm quite certain my accent gave that away. I'm the owner of a restaurant in London and, at Walter's request, the ship's chef for the second time on this yacht and, as fate would have it, my best friend from sophomore year in San Francisco when I was on an exchange is standing next to me. We haven't seen each other in for ever, so there's a lot of catching up to do.'

The group all then looked at Libby. Daniel could not avoid doing the same. He could not help but notice she nervously but purposely made eye contact with them all but not with him. He could also not help but notice that she was as beautiful as he remembered, perhaps even more so. Her stunning red hair was tied away from her face in a ponytail. He recalled it flowing across the white pillowcase as she lay naked beside him in the warmth of her bed.

He dug his fingers into his palms, trying to keep his mind from wandering back to that time. He couldn't let the memories overtake him. He had to stay on task. Thinking even for the briefest moment of the way it had been would be pointless. He could not change what had happened or make amends. She was angry and hurt even after all the time that had passed and she had every right to feel that way, although he thought she would have moved on by now and not reacted the way she had when she'd seen him. Perhaps—and understandably—she would have been cold and distant but her reaction was more than that. He had never made contact, never written or called so he had given her no reason to think of him.

'Elizabeth McDonald, but I prefer to be called Libby, and I'm from Oakland, which is about twenty minutes outside of San Francisco. I have nursing experience in both A&E and Cardiology and recently I was one of Sir Walter's nurses pre- and post-operatively. And, this is my first time on a ship.'

The group all smiled back. All except Daniel. His look was sombre and he didn't take his eyes off Libby. He couldn't. He was momentarily caught up in thoughts of the past. Daniel knew he had to get a grip on his feelings. Something tugged at his heart as he stood watching her from across the room and it scared him to the core.

Daniel Dimosa had a battle with his feelings on his hands.

'Okay, I guess now we know a little about each other and too much about Boris and... I've forgotten the other one's name already,' Eric said in a light-hearted manner.

'Molly,' Steve interjected. 'And to think I was going to give you one of their pups.'

'No, please, that's not necessary. In fact, my wife would be mortified by the thought,' Eric said, shaking his head. 'So, let's get down to the briefing. You know most of it but it's regulation to go over it so I will, particularly as a few of you are new to this particular ship. The previous voyages of the *Coral Contessa* have been without incident and I hope this trip will be the same.

'We're on a US-owned ship sailing in international waters. In keeping with guidelines, all staff are on call twenty-four hours a day. You will be assigned eight-hour shifts but you will have a pager in case you're needed twenty-four hours a day. It is not to be switched off at any time and I expect that you report here immediately if called. Neither Steve nor I will call unless it's an emergency. There's always the chance we could find ourselves in a situation where we need additional support or we may need your assistance to help seriously sick or injured patients to disembark so I need to know I can always reach you.

'Georgie is fluent in French and Italian, Stacey in Spanish, and I also speak a little Greek so we should be able to assist Sir Walter's international guests according to the information I was provided. Oh, and Steve is fluent in golden retriever but we won't be needing that on this trip.'

The team laughed, except for Libby. She stood staring into space, not capable of reacting, and Daniel understood why. She was feeling trapped and, while it wasn't his fault, Daniel felt guilty. Her distaste at being in the same space as him was understandable.

He watched as Georgie leaned over and gave her a hug. There was a very real bond between Libby and Georgie and one that, it appeared, had not diminished despite their years apart. He was not surprised because Libby was hard to forget. She was genuine and compassionate and so much more he didn't want to remember, but all of it was coming back to him at lightning speed.

CHAPTER FIVE

'SIR WALTER AND his remaining guests are due to arrive shortly. His grandson and guest arrived early and have already boarded and are in their stateroom. We are scheduled to set sail at fifteen hundred hours,' the Captain announced. 'So please take this time to get to know your way around your home away from home and meet the rest of the crew who have been on board for quite a few hours, some since yesterday, in preparation for the voyage.'

Daniel was still coming to terms with the situation. It was surreal seeing Libby and he had to keep reminding himself that after this week he would never see her again. Their paths would never cross. There was nothing to bind them together and everything to keep them apart. He had to make sure he did not let old feelings creep into the present. He could not truly make amends and he did not want to lie or hurt her further. She had made it clear she wanted their time together to pass quickly and she was only here because she had no other option. How he wanted it to be different but that wasn't in the stars for them.

The senior crew were dispersing but Daniel needed to speak with Libby about Walter's condition and in general about her role on the yacht, and after that he would keep his word and restrict all interactions to a professional minimum.

'Libby, can you please stay back?' Daniel asked. 'I would like to clarify a few things as this is your first time as a ship's nurse.'

Libby paused in mid-step and turned back. Daniel could see by her expression her distaste of the idea.

'Do you want me to stay too?' Georgie asked in a lowered voice.

'I'm good, Georgie, thank you,' she said softly. 'I'm sure this won't take long and then I'll head back to my cabin.'

'Five minutes, tops,' Daniel responded, making it clear he had heard both of them.

Georgie walked away, leaving Daniel and Libby alone for the second time that day. Libby crossed her arms and glared in silence at him. Her hostile body language told him everything he already knew.

'Libby,' he began. 'I will keep this very brief, but I do need to explain what we do and don't have access to on the yacht in regard to providing treatment to Walter and any other passengers.'

'I'm quite happy to go and find that out for myself,' she retorted as she paced the deck.

'I'm sure you could do that but it might be more efficient if I was to give you a brief overview because we don't know what the next few days might hold in terms of Walter's health. What we do know is that we have an almost eighty-year-old man who has undergone a triple coronary artery bypass graft and insists on behaving as if he has never seen the inside of an operating theatre. You and I are both aware that he is not fully recovered and he is as stubborn as the next billionaire and believes he knows best in every aspect of his life...' Daniel's words were cut short by the arrival of a uniformed young man.

'I'm Stan, one of the stewards, and I need you to come quickly. There's a young woman on the top deck. She gashed her head and one of the stewardesses is sitting with her. There's a load of blood.'

'Let's go,' Daniel said, immediately following the young man.

'I'm coming too,' Libby answered.

Within moments, the three of them climbed the circular staircase leading to the top deck to find a young woman dressed in shorts and a bikini top sitting in a deck chair. A stewardess stood beside her, holding a blood-soaked white hand-towel against the young woman's forehead. She had visible injuries, including grazes and cuts to the exposed skin on her shoulders, upper arms and face. There was a first-aid kit lying nearby.

'Do you know what happened… Rose?' Daniel asked as scanned the stewardess's name tag.

'Natalie had a tumble on the top deck,' Rose replied matter-of-factly. 'One of the engineers found her. It looks like she fell from the climbing wall, which had been cordoned off as it was unattended, and she had been on it without a harness. I asked her not to move; I thought she might have neck injuries. I've done first aid and knew she should remain still and wait for you as she might need a neck brace but she ignored my instructions.

'She climbed to her feet and then collapsed back down in the chair. I brought the first-aid kit up with me when I was called.'

'Do you know if she was conscious when she was found?'

'No, they said she was unresponsive. The

engineer initially thought she had hit her head and been killed in the fall,' Rose told him. 'Poor man, he was quite shaken up by it.'

Daniel took a pair of disposable gloves from the open first-aid kit and Libby followed suit, slipping on a pair and moving closer to the young woman.

'I can take over and give your hand a rest,' she told Rose as her gloved hand replaced the stewardess's and held the bloodied towel in place.

'Natalie,' Daniel began, looking directly at the young patient. 'I'm a doctor, my name is Daniel and this is Libby, the ship's nurse. We need to take a closer look at your injuries.'

'It's not that bad,' the young woman mumbled. 'I just need to wash up and have some painkillers for my head…and I'll be fine. Honest I will.'

'I think you'll need a bit more than that, Natalie,' Daniel said firmly before turning to the stewardess. 'Thank you, Rose. Libby and I have got this. We can take it from here.'

Her reaction to hearing the words from Daniel took Libby by surprise. They reminded her of how Daniel would say that in ER. 'Libby and I have got this,' he'd said more times than she could remember…or cared to remember at this time. They had been such a great team. Everyone had recognised how well they'd meshed on the job. They thought the same way, Libby pre-empting what Daniel would need. There had been an unspoken trust. They had worked like a hand and glove... Libby just wished it had been the same in their personal lives.

'We haven't even set sail yet, so it's not a good omen for the rest of the trip,' Rose commented before leaving the area. The young woman was still sitting upright but swaying a little. On closer inspection, Libby could see there were deep grazes to her elbows and knees with trickles of blood on her left leg. Her right slip-on-style shoe was missing but as Libby's eyes darted around, there was no sign of it close by.

'I'm going to carefully take the towel away from your head so we can look at the wound,' Libby told her softly to allay any fear. Libby had stepped into medical mode and made a conscious decision to leave their personal issues behind.

The young woman remained very still as Libby released the towel. She knew immediately it was a deep wound and would require stitches or else there would be an unattractive scar running across the victim's forehead above her left eye. Some of Natalie's blonde hair was matted into the bloodied area. The length of time between the fall and being found might have been more than first thought.

'It appears the bleeding has ceased for the time being at least,' Daniel told Libby as he leaned in and examined the wound very closely. The scent of his musky cologne filled her senses and her immediate reaction was to pull away but she couldn't. She was still supporting the young woman so she had to stay closer to Daniel than she'd ever thought she would again. She swallowed and tried to calm her racing heart. It wasn't anger surging through her veins. It was something she had forgotten how to feel.

'She will need stitches,' Libby remarked in a tone that gave away nothing of how she was feeling.

'I agree,' Daniel responded. 'However, I would suggest that since it's in a prominent place on your face, a plastic surgeon would be your best option.'

The young woman nodded but appeared unperturbed with the news about her face.

'I'm just going to check your pulse,' Libby cut in.

'I need to ask you some questions while Nurse McDonald takes your observations.

'What is your name and date of birth?'
Daniel went on.

'Natalie.' The young woman paused and
looked up, her eyes darting about as if searching for the words. 'Natalie, Natalie... Martin.'

'And how old are you?' Daniel asked, not
taking his eyes away from his young patient
as he observed her reactions.

'I'm eighteen...no, no, I'm nineteen,' she
told him as she reached up to the wound area
with her blood-stained fingers.

Gently but firmly Daniel directed her hand
away from the wound. 'Your hands are con-
taminated. You need to refrain from touch-
ing the wound until it's dressed.'

'Can you please tell me today's date and
the day of the week?' Libby asked.

'Monday, June tenth.'

Libby looked at Daniel. It was Sunday,
June eleventh. The woman was lucid but still
a little disoriented.

'Natalie, are you in significant pain anywhere other than your forehead and the
scratches on your legs?' Daniel asked as he
reached for a stethoscope.

'It kind of hurts all over but if you can
clean me up and give me some strong painkillers I'll be okay.'

'Pulse is seventy,' Libby announced.

'Is that good or bad?'

'Your observations are good, Natalie, but it's not as simple as a strong pulse and a few painkillers. I need to better understand how you're feeling as there can be underlying issues from a significant fall. Is there any significant targeted pain or generally a battered and bruised feeling?' Daniel continued the line of questioning. Libby was aware he was not convinced that the injuries from the fall were as clear cut as they could see.

Natalie's loss of consciousness for a still undetermined period of time and a fall from a height were concerning him. He was a thorough doctor and not one to compromise a patient's health care so he was taking his time and remaining calm. He always had.

'The back of my head is the worst,' she said very slowly, purposely rolling her head in a circular motion. 'But a shot or two tonight and I'll be fine.'

'Best not to move your head that way, and I might remind you that at nineteen you're underage and would not be served alcohol on this ship. Please stay as still as possible and let me look at the back of your head,' Daniel said as he walked to the other side of the examination table and carefully checked the posterior skull region.

'As I suspected, there is an area of your skull that is somewhat depressed. For a conclusive prognosis we will need to do X-rays and you're going to need to be in hospital under observation.'

'For how long?'

'Overnight at least. I'm not sure how far you fell and for how long you were unconscious. Both are concerning me.'

Libby began to clean the wound. Careful not to dislodge the blood clot, she freed some of the matted hair and applied an antiseptic solution and sterile gauze dressing. Daniel reached over and his hand brushed hers lightly as he held the dressing in place while she reached for a soft wrap bandage.

'I'll wrap the wound,' she began, trying to steady her breathing. Even through the gloves she had felt the warmth of his hand on hers and she was surprised at her reaction. 'I don't want to use anything adhesive on her skin.'

'Good call,' Daniel replied.

The young woman was agitated but staying still enough to allow Libby to dress the wound.

'Can the plastic surgeon come on board to see me?'

'No, Natalie, the only course of action now is to clean up the wound, give you a temporary dressing and then arrange for you to disembark and transfer immediately to the local hospital. I would prefer that you are transported in an ambulance so I will make a call now and arrange for that. They may have a plastic surgeon on staff at the hospital or refer you to one. I'm not conversant with the local hospital's scope.'

'I'm not leaving,' she announced loudly. 'I'm going to the engagement party with my boyfriend, Ernest. You know, Walter's his great-uncle and he owns this yacht. You can't force me to leave.'

'I'm sorry, Natalie, but that's exactly what I'm doing and I can guarantee you that Sir Walter will not argue the point,' Daniel responded. His voice was firm but not at the volume of hers. 'It's not in your best interest to remain on board with your injuries. You need to get to the nearest hospital as soon as possible for a complete assessment…and I mean as soon as possible.

'Head injuries are not to be taken lightly— the extent of your injuries from the fall may not become obvious immediately and the damage to your skull is concerning me. There's a risk of internal bleeding. You need a CAT scan and may be admitted to the intensive care unit dependent upon the results.

While you feel fine now, don't be cavalier about the seriousness of the fall.'

'Cava what?'

'Cavalier. It means don't dismiss how serious the injury could be,' Libby explained.

'But Ernest can watch me and tell you if there's anything wrong.'

Daniel reached for the ship's phone. 'We might well be out at sea when either of you notice a problem. And that would be too late.'

'There's a helipad. I can get taken back to shore anytime.'

'While there is a helipad, there's not a helicopter on board. You could lapse into a coma without warning and it would be too late to call for the coastguard and I'm not prepared to take that chance with your life.'

'Are you serious? A coma?'

'Yes, there's always a risk, however slight, with a severe blow to the head of what we call extradural blueing from the middle meningeal artery or one of its branches and as a result a haemorrhage inside your skull. I understand it's all medical jargon to you, but I'm letting you know that it has the potential to be serious. Your well-being is my priority, Natalie, not your social life. Take another trip with Ernest, but next time don't climb an unattended rock wall.'

* * *

Ten minutes later Libby watched as paramedics arrived and secured Natalie on the barouche in preparation for the ambulance trip to the Western Miami General Hospital. Daniel provided them with the background and a copy of the medical notes that Libby had taken during the examination.

Ernest had come to say goodbye but he had chosen to remain on board. He told her not to worry and that she would be fine. He'd have shots in her honour at the party and send selfies to her. Libby could see the young woman's disappointment and anxiety about being transported to hospital was heightened by the sadness of doing it alone. Her boyfriend had chosen partying with his family over her and that had to hurt. Particularly at nineteen.

'Thank you for your assistance, Libby.'

Libby nodded to Daniel and turned to leave. Her work was done. Now she knew she needed distance more than ever.

'I will be suggesting tighter controls over the management of the climbing wall. I might suggest it's closed altogether unless there's someone experienced managing it twenty-four seven. Perhaps I'll speak to the chief stewardess and ascertain the number of young people on board who may be tempted to do something similar. I don't think there're any others but I'd rather be safe than sorry.'

'That's a sensible idea,' she said, not wanting to remain near him even a moment longer. She admired him immensely as a doctor and she worried that might somehow influence how she felt about him as a man. It had once before. From the first day Daniel had stepped into the Northern Bay General Hospital A&E where Libby had been nursing, she had been drawn to him, and history was at risk of repeating itself.

He was a skilled and knowledgeable doctor and she had adored working with him as she'd felt that every moment she did so she learned more and became a better nurse. He had taken the time to explain procedures and the reason for his diagnoses, prognoses and treatment plans, however unconventional or, at times, unpopular they might have seemed. He was thorough and methodical, leaving nothing to chance. He was also very handsome and charismatic and none of that had changed.

An empathetic bedside manner was not at the forefront on this occasion but it was understandable. Daniel wanted what was best for the young woman, and wasn't about to be swayed by her pleas. He didn't mind being the bad guy in her opinion if it meant saving her life—or at the very least keeping her pretty face from being disfigured by ugly scarring.

But Libby had to save herself from being drawn back in. She had to get away as quickly as she could because she could not afford to be swept away by her feelings.

Forgetting the past was not an option and she could not let his professional abilities overshadow the ruin he had left in his wake and the decision that still weighed heavily on her mind. She walked away from Daniel without another word.

Libby arrived back at the cabin and found Georgie waiting outside her door. She gave her the abbreviated version of the events with the climbing incident as they stepped inside.

'I wondered what took you so long. I thought it might have been a heart-to-heart with Daniel,' Georgie said as she leaned against the bathroom door.

Libby was in the tiny space, washing her hands, and shook her head. 'Not interested. That time has passed. He's had years to reach out and explain what happened and he didn't. I'm done wanting to know.'

'Good for you. There's plenty of fish in the sea and the Caribbean is the perfect place to go fishing. Speaking of that, how about we step out and have a quick look around the yacht? I've done all the prep in the galley for tonight's dinner, which is a seafood buffet, and I've left it with the other two crew members who can manage for the next hour or so. I'll head back and put the finishing touches to it and make the dessert later. We can find somewhere to sit and enjoy a little sun. Walter wouldn't mind at all. Believe me, if he's fed well—and he will be—then all will be well in the world.'

'I'm not really in the mood, but you go,' Libby replied, deep in thought as she made her way to her still unpacked suitcase for a clean top. She had noticed a few tiny spots of blood on the one she was wearing. 'I don't want to ruin your fun.'

Socialising was the last thing on her mind. She felt like a prisoner in a glamorous floating penitentiary and wondered how she would stay sane for the next few days. No matter what she'd said to Georgie, in her heart it wasn't over and she found her mind wandering to thoughts of him and their time together...and to the son they shared.

The brief time tending to Natalie together had made it all so real again. Everything that she had struggled to forget was returning as vividly as the day it had happened. The good, the wonderful, the exciting, all of it, along with the heartache and the confusion. It was overwhelming her.

Without thinking, she reached for her pendant. Her every reason for living was her son and she was not yet ready to share that secret with Daniel. He was a man who could sweep her off her feet, make her feel like she was so special and then disappear overnight without an explanation. Daniel was a brilliant doctor but Billy deserved more than that. He deserved stability and a loving father who would not disappear on an unexplained whim.

There was also the niggling question of whether, upon learning he was a father, Daniel might demand shared custody and Libby had no idea where Daniel lived. That was something that Libby had neither the funds nor the emotional strength to fight. She just needed time to decide whether Billy would be better off with Daniel in his life and, if so, when she would tell him.

There was much that Daniel would have to explain and prove for her to make such a huge decision and she worried that seven days and nights might not be a long enough time. Libby felt certain that if it wasn't for them being on the ship together, he would not have given her another thought.

She just wished she felt the same.

'You can't turn into a hermit because of Daniel,' Georgie said firmly. 'We've known each other since we were sixteen and you haven't changed. You're so sweet and lovely and I don't want to see you lock yourself away because of him.'

'That's not the reason…'

'Libby.' Georgie looked at her friend. 'That's a porky pie and we both know it.'

Libby frowned in Georgie's direction with no clue what her friend was talking about.

'A porky pie is a lie,' she continued, without Libby responding. It was a lie. Daniel was the reason for her simmering anxiety and her lack of enthusiasm about everything, except getting off the ship. Disembarking the *Coral Contessa* was the one thing she was looking forward to very much but she knew something had to be resolved one way or the other before she did.

'Libby, I didn't mean to be rude or forward in any way. I just meant that you're making up an excuse not to get out and about because of whatever happened between you and Daniel. But locking yourself in the cabin won't change anything. All it will do is waste the experience of your first time on a yacht.'

'Maybe I'm making an excuse but it's complicated, Georgie, and…to be honest, I guess I'm still in shock. I never thought I'd see him again in my life.'

'Your fainting made it very clear that even hearing his name was a huge surprise and not a pleasant one. It's always complicated when men are involved. They generally manage to make a complete mess of things most of the time.'

'More than you know.'

'I guessed it didn't end well and, again, I'm not prying. You can share as much or as little as you want with me, but I'm going to share some things I know about the man.'

'Things you know about him? What things?'

'Daniel is handsome and could have pretty much any woman he wanted within ten miles of the ship but from what I've heard from the other crew members he's single and has never become involved with anyone he works with and that's not because there haven't been offers. Passengers and crew alike literally throw themselves at him, but he keeps his distance.'

'How do you know this?'

'Ships' doctors don't exist in huge numbers, and Stacey and one of my galley crew have worked with him before on larger cruise ships. It's a tight-knit community and someone as handsome and eligible as Daniel is fodder for gossip. Only there isn't any about him. He's the ultimate elusive bachelor and a gentleman. His liaisons, and there will be some, no doubt, must be fleeting and kept ashore and discreet with no drama. He's never married and he's quite private about his personal life and his family, if he has any, but he's an amazing doctor and a good and fair colleague. That's it.'

'That's a lot of background,' Libby said, still uneasy about how quickly the crew of the *Coral Contessa* had updated Georgie about Daniel. All the more reason to keep her secret safe. That would no doubt spread like wildfire and she didn't need that. Her anxiety was suddenly on the rise again.

'He's squeaky clean and that makes him even more desirable…and almost a celebrity. There are a lot of Latin lovers at sea, but he's not one of them.'

'No offence, Georgie, but I don't think I want to hear any more. I'm not ready to hear wonderful character references about my ex,' Libby said as she sat down on the bunk and slumped back against her pillows.

'I don't know how to make you feel better

about the situation, Libby. I told you what I know so you can feel better about yourself. By your reaction you were clearly in love with the man and I wanted you to know, whatever happened, he's a decent man so your instincts when you fell for him were right.'

Libby closed her eyes and wished she could open them and find herself in her own bed in her own house and not staring at the lower deck of a yacht about to sail through the Caribbean. She should have paid more attention to her initial doubts about the trip and fought harder not to be sent on an adventure at sea. The reality was closer to a disaster.

'I know your intentions are good and I appreciate what you're trying to do but I don't trust my instincts about much right now.'

'Then trust mine,' Georgie said as she stepped closer again. 'You can't change anything except yourself into a swimsuit. Let's get some sun while we can. There's another few hours before Sir Walter's guests claim the sundecks for their own.'

'Like I said, you go. I'd rather stay here and call home.'

'Call home while I slip into my swimsuit and then we'll go for a walk at least. Wallowing inside your cabin won't change anything. The sun at least has a chance to change your mood and lift your spirits, so let's give it a chance. We need to relax with a fruit cocktail, non-alcoholic of course since we're working, but maybe later tonight we can switch it up for a champagne. It's not often you find your-self at sea with your absolute best friend who you haven't seen in over a decade.'

CHAPTER SIX

'Isn't the sun glorious?' Georgie asked her reluctant companion. 'The view's stunning and we haven't even set sail yet. I think we're going to have a lovely time.'

'Mmm,' Libby responded, staring straight ahead as the two strolled around the deck. She had called home and spoken to Billy and her mother and everything was fine. Billy was about to have lunch and then help his grandfather build a big red racing-car bed. Her parents were spoiling their grandson and he was clearly so excited about sleeping in a racing car that night that he didn't have too much time to talk to her. Knowing that Billy was happy and not missing her was a relief.

She had changed into white shorts and a navy striped T-shirt. Georgie was in a pink and green floral bathing suit but Libby had no intention of baring that much skin. Knowing that Daniel was on board was making her self-conscious, not to mention that Bradley had packed the skimpiest of bikinis in her suitcase.

The crew were busily preparing for the final passengers yet to arrive and tending to the needs of those already on board. Sir Walter was the most important passenger and he was yet to arrive. Libby had not seen him since he had been discharged from hospital a week after his surgery and she was genuinely looking forward to seeing him again. If only it were under different circumstances.

'I'll take "mmm" for the moment but by tomorrow I'll be looking for a smidgen more enthusiasm.'

'That might be my limit, I'm sorry,' Libby said as she drew breath, unable to forget for even an instant that Daniel was at any time only a deck away from her. The thought of him was making her heart and her body react in ways that made her very uneasy. It was the most confused she had been in four years.

Georgie returned a half-smile and Libby suddenly felt pangs of guilt. Her behaviour was less than gracious after Georgie's earlier excitement to see her and the support she had shown when she'd needed it most. Libby knew she needed to lighten up. She had agreed, albeit reluctantly and under du-

ress, to be on board for the next seven days…
or six and a half, she told herself as the first
day was almost half-gone.

'I'm sorry, let's walk around and find a
seat in the sun. You're right, it will be lovely.'

After just over an hour of Miami sunshine,
incessant chatter and a delicious pineapple
smoothie each, Georgie excused herself to
return to galley duties. Libby was returning
to her cabin to change into her uniform when
a steward caught up with her.

'Sir Walter has just boarded and wants to
see you.'

'He's early. I didn't think we would see him
for another hour and I haven't changed into
my uniform.'

'He won't mind, I'm sure,' he told her as
he led the way to their host, who was making himself comfortable on a sun lounger on
the deck at the bow of the yacht. He had an
entourage of people with him but, as Libby
quickly and thankfully noticed, no Daniel.

'Hello, Nurse Elizabeth. It's lovely to see
you again, my dear. I hope you're not upset
that I kidnapped you for a few days?'

'Hello, Sir Walter. I'm happy to be here,'
she lied. While lying was not a habit of hers,
it was not Sir Walter's fault that his yacht

was the last place on earth she wanted to be. She wanted to appear gracious and not dampen his excitement about the cruise and his daughter's engagement party. 'I just want to keep you on your path to a full recovery on this cruise.' That was not a lie. That was Libby's sole focus. Daniel was not a focus of hers. Although avoiding him was.

'We'll see about that.' He laughed. 'You see, I'm going to enjoy what time I have left on earth and not fuss too much with healthy hoo-ha. If I want a beef Wellington with gravy then I shall have one, and I do not like exercise. At all.'

Libby knew she would have her hands full with Sir Walter. It appeared that both men of significance on the *Coral Contessa* were going to challenge her reserves.

She just needed to dig deep and rise to the occasion.

'So now we've caught up, why don't you take a look around my little yacht, make sure you know where everything is and I can sit here and catch up with my friends. I'm feeling as fit as a bull and I don't need you…'

'Are you sure?'

'Couldn't be more sure,' he told her. 'And I know you have one of those pager things,

laque caused by a diet high in an-
fined sugar, smoking, inactivity
ve alcohol. And you're indulging
again!'

ted her chin defiantly as Walter
at her, taking his time to reply.
each was staring the other down,
he prelude to a gunfight.

ther silly nor reckless in spend-
he I have left sailing, young lady.
and the Caribbean are the clos-
being with my beloved late wife,
he was the love of my life and if
be while I feel close to her. I told
when I held her hand as she died
she will hold mine in the bow of
I die on it.'

s taken aback at the emotion in
e sentiment in his words and the
ng in the corners of his weary
oftened her tone but kept reso-
nessage. 'I do understand what
g and how you're feeling, Wal-
don't have to die anytime soon.
l as much as you like and feel
beloved wife for many years to
u must stop smoking and drink-
quor.'

ybe I don't want to live a great

so someone will find you, or the doc, if I my
ticker starts acting up.'

Libby left Walter and his group, and took an
unaccompanied tour of the yacht. It was magnificent on every one of the four decks, all of
which were serviced by a glass elevator. The
decor was like that of an Italian hotel from a
magazine, with white marble floors, ornate
gilded furnishings and a ceiling in the formal dining area that was reminiscent of the
Sistine Chapel.

As she passed one of the two oversized
columns near the bar, a steward pushed on
a small panel and to Libby's surprise the entire column opened and she saw it was filled
with shelves of polished crystal glasses and
decanters. Opulence was the word that came
to mind everywhere she looked. She'd had
no idea what a yacht of that much splendour
would be worth but she knew she couldn't
earn enough in a million lifetimes to buy one.
Libby looked around, knowing she had something far more valuable in her life. Something
money could never buy. She had her son.

After roaming for a little while longer
and stumbling across the room towards the
bow of the yacht, which housed a speedboat
and two jet-skis, Libby thought she had seen

enough. A boat on a yacht was too much for her so she made her way to her cabin to shower and change into one of the uniforms that had been hanging in the wardrobe. She pulled her slightly damp hair into a low bun at the nape of her neck and checked her appearance in the mirror on the back of her cabin door. Libby was very conscious that she wanted to appear professional and there to do her job.

It was a message she wanted to send to everyone. Including Daniel.

Libby returned to find Walter with a lit cigar in one hand and a short crystal glass of what she felt certain was whiskey over ice in the other hand. She could not mask being upset to see him smoking and drinking. She was disappointed and angry in equal amounts and suspected that was why he had sent her on a sightseeing trip around the yacht. He was completely disregarding everything he had been told in hospital before and after his bypass surgery.

He had been warned that smoking could increase his chance of blood clots and he risked a serious chest infection along with a slower healing process. It was behaviour far more dangerous than consuming a beef Welling-

ton and she intended t_____
she thought.

'Sir Walter—' she _____
her voice not maskin_____
uation.

'Walter, remembe_____
Walter,' he returned _____
wide-brimmed hat h_____

'Fine, I will call y_____
I want you to put t_____
down now. You can_____
ing after your heart_____

Walter stared bac_____
didn't care if he fir_____
be a blessing but it_____
telling him off. Ke_____
sisting him back t_____
cared about.

'I'm going to b_____
into his eyes. 'Wh_____
behaviour and you_____
weeks out from m_____
life and you're sai_____
smoking and drin_____
ager. You've cor_____
as your nurse and_____
silly behaviour o_____
stand around an_____
won't. The walls_____

with fa_____
imal fa_____
and exc_____
in all of_____

Libby_____
looked _____
It was a_____
not unli_____

'I am _____
ing what_____
This yac_____
est I get _____
Contessa_____
I go, it w_____
her as mu_____
and I kno_____
this yacht_____

Libby _____
his voice,_____
tears form_____
eyes. She _____
lute in her_____
you're say_____
ter, but yo_____
You can s_____
close to yo_____
come but y_____
ing heavy l_____

'Well, m_____

many years,' he retorted, turning away from her. 'Maybe I'm lonely and tired and I want to enjoy what little time I have left, and if I hasten the end, then so be it.'

'Please forgive me for saying this, but I think that's being quite disrespectful.'

'Disrespectful? And to whom am I being disrespectful?' His head turned back to Libby, his eyes wide and his lips cutting a thin line in his clearly irritated face.

'To the doctors and theatre nurses who saved your life.'

'They're paid to do that. It's their job, just like it's your job to take care of me for the next week so I make it to my niece's engagement. Not that I completely approve of her fiancé but nonetheless you and the doc will keep me alive to see that day.'

'And what about the day after?' Libby said, taking the empty seat beside him. One of the family entourage had quickly moved away when the polite but somewhat heated discussion had erupted. 'What about living to see her children, your great-nieces and-nephews? To bounce them on your knee and look into their gorgeous cherub faces. Don't you want to live to do that?'

'Using unborn children to get your point across,' he said butting his cigar on the ashtray nearby. 'Now, that's hitting below the belt.'

'I'll do whatever it takes, Walter, to make you see reason. You've survived a massive operation and now it's up to you to take care of yourself and since you're from the UK, if you do as your medical team say you may even make a hundred and receive a letter from the Queen. Wouldn't that make your day? You could frame the letter and hang it in your suite or perhaps behind the bar for everyone to see.'

'Using Her Majesty now. To what ends will you go? Have you no shame, Libby?'

'No shame at all when it comes to your health. I will do and say whatever I must to keep you healthy.'

'Well, the whole hundredth birthday and the Queen won't work,' he argued with a raised eyebrow. 'My hundredth birthday is twenty-one years away so I'm sure if I make it that far it won't be the Queen who'll be writing to me. She'll be in a better place by then.'

'The reigning monarch, then,' Libby cut in. 'Does it matter who signs the letter from Buckingham Palace? Let's just get you to the age to qualify first.'

'Lovely thought, but I'm painfully aware that while the survival rate for bypass patients who make it to five weeks after the operation is pretty darn good, everything changes after about seven or eight years. The chance of me falling off my perch jumps considerably so I'll be lucky to see my ninetieth birthday let alone my hundredth. Anyway, I've decided I'm going to damn well enjoy the next few years and leave the rest to fate. I'm most certainly not going to spend what years I have left sitting in an armchair, looking out of a bay window with a mohair rug on my knees…and a cup of Earl Grey tea in my hand.'

'With all due respect, Walter, there's quite a lot of space between a nursing home and smoking cigars and drinking whiskey in this very ornate floating bar.'

Walter eyed Libby in silence again. His lips once again formed a hard line in his wrinkled face but he didn't look annoyed. She couldn't read his expression at all. Libby knew she should never play poker with him as he was giving nothing away. Her stomach suddenly dropped.

Had she gone too far? She really liked Walter but she couldn't sit by and watch him risk his health unnecessarily, but neither did she want to appear unprofessional and cross the line. Under his gruff exterior, he was a kind and generous man and, quite apart from her duty of care as a nurse, she had grown fond of him while he had been in her care in hospital. She wanted to see him live as many years as he could and not throw them away on cigars and alcohol.

His lips turned to a smirk as he grudgingly placed his glass on the table.

'I like you, young lady. You have what I think you Americans called *spunk* and what we British call unbridled determination. Some might even call it stubbornness, but a word of warning: I too have stubbornness in bucketloads. It's how I built my empire and I'm not going to roll over and play dead anytime soon. You'll have your hands full if you think I'm going to change my ways easily.'

Libby climbed to her feet. She'd been worried that she had overstepped the mark but by his tone and the fact he'd said he liked her, clearly she hadn't said too much.

'I'm up for the challenge, Walter.'

'And what challenge would that be?'

Libby turned to see Daniel standing far too close for her liking and quickly she turned her face back to her patient. Her heart had instantly picked up speed and she hated herself for the way she was reacting. She should be angry whenever she saw him. Furious, in fact. But she wasn't.

Her body had no shame, she realised. Immediately upon hearing the timbre of his voice or seeing his tall, dark silhouette or when the scent of his cologne overtook her senses, she lost all reason and self-respect. And Daniel's effect on her wasn't lessening in impact. She had already witnessed how handsome he looked in his crisp white uniform with its stark contrast to his tanned Mediterranean skin. She didn't need to look at him again and be reminded of that. Everything about him and the way he made her feel frightened her.

She was just grateful that all of what she was thinking and feeling was not obvious to anyone else.

'It appears, Daniel, that Libby thinks she can change my *reckless* ways and make me see a ripe old age so I can get a letter from Buckingham Palace,' Walter told him with a wink. 'But I'm trying to tell her that it's pointless to try to change a man. Once we're out of nappies, or diapers as the Americans call them, no woman can change us. It's really quite pointless to try, don't you agree?'

Libby closed her eyes. The words resonated in her heart. Daniel, she suspected, was a man who didn't want to change. He was a man who was happy with the way he lived his life. Loving and leaving women with no thought for the hurt he caused or the hearts he broke.

'I believe, Walter, that under the right circumstances and with the right incentive, a man can change.'

Libby was taken aback by Daniel's answer to Walter's question. *The right incentive?* Did that mean she hadn't been incentive enough for him to change his philandering ways all those years ago? And what did he mean by the right circumstances? She was terribly confused and she felt anger starting to brew deep inside. Strangely, she liked the feeling of anger. It gave her perspective and control over the situation.

'Codswallop!' Walter bellowed. 'That's all New Age, politically correct codswallop. I have no intention of changing my ways, no matter how sweet or how pretty the messenger may be.'

Libby shook her head at the backhanded compliment as she refused to look in Daniel's direction. She didn't want to see the reaction on his face.

'Let's not debate whether men can change,' Libby suddenly interjected to put the con-

versation, and her thoughts, back on a professional level. 'Let's get back to the issue at
hand. Your health and the responsibility of
your ship's medical team.'

'Let me see if I have this correctly. I'm
paying you both very well—not to mention
handsomely donating to a hospital in San
Francisco—to have you accompany me on
this trip with the sole purpose of preventing
me from having fun and reprimanding me at
every available opportunity?'

'No.' Daniel stepped closer as he spoke.
'Walter, Libby and I are here to ensure you
have the best chance of a full recovery. You
must understand that the surgery you un-
derwent is not a cure for coronary heart disease. It's a second chance if you change your
ways, but if you don't you will be right back
to square one in a very short period of time
and we don't want that.'

'Oh, dear, I have no chance here. You're
both singing from the same hymn sheet,' he
said with an expression of defeat crossing his
face. 'Fine, I will refrain from my wicked
ways for the next week but after that, when
you two are out of my sight, all bets are off.
I will do as you ask for the next week purely
because I can't handle seven days of incessant nagging…in stereo.'

With that he stood up and stretched his back from side to side. 'I think I will have a nice shower and change for dinner. Georgie is preparing some of my favourite food and I intend to enjoy it...without a cigar or whiskey, as ordered by my keepers, but I'll damn well have dessert if I fancy it. And if either of you try to stop me, I'll have you thrown overboard and you'll be swimming with the fish tonight.'

Daniel smirked and Libby's lips formed a half-smile as Walter left. Suddenly his entourage followed suit and dispersed, leaving Libby and Daniel standing together.

Libby looked out to sea for a moment before she began to walk away. Being alone with Daniel as the sun began to set was a recipe for disaster. The setting was far too romantic and she knew, despite all the unanswered questions and her simmering anger, there was the smallest chance that she might still be vulnerable to him.

And she could not afford to go down that path again. There was so much more at stake this time.

'Please don't go, Libby,' he began. 'I know I said I'd find a way to ensure we're not working together but perhaps we could sit and talk sometime. I do think fondly of the time we spent together.'

'Not fondly enough to get in touch any time over the last four years,' she spat back at him coldly.

CHAPTER SEVEN

'Mr Hudson.' Libby addressed the man she
had directed to follow her inside the makeshift infirmary. She paused as she closed the
door. 'Please come in.'

'It would be my pleasure,' he told her, then
continued, 'But you can call me Maxwell.'

Libby drew a short breath. His response
had been followed by a peculiar stare in her
direction. Her intuition was telling her that
Maxwell's gaze was not purely patient-nurse.
His eyes seemed to hover on her lips, not
meeting her eyes at all. It was odd but she
shrugged it off. Maybe his hearing was com-
promised and he was lip reading. Some of
the older patients she had cared for over the
years did that, although Maxwell appeared to
be in his late forties but she couldn't be sure.
He was not particularly tall and quite stocky
in build, with a receding hairline so his age
was difficult to pinpoint.

'Please sit down,' she said, motioning towards the chair adjacent to the cabin desk as she stepped inside the en suite bathroom and washed her hands. 'The doctor is not available, but I can take some notes and see what the issue is and call for him if there's anything urgent. He isn't too far away.' Just far enough to allow her to feel more comfortable.

'He can't go too far—we're on a ship. Unless he jumps overboard and then it would just be you and me.'

His response was odd and made her feel uncomfortable. And the way he was looking at her when she reappeared with freshly scrubbed hands even more so.

'It was a joke,' he said with a snigger and a raised eyebrow. Still standing a little too close for Libby's liking, he continued, 'I'm sure he wouldn't jump off the ship—at least not while you're on here.'

Libby was not impressed but was determined to remain professional and move past the blatant flirting.

'What appears to be your problem today?' Libby asked in a monotone.

Maxwell stared at her in silence, his eyebrow still arched.

'Is everything all right, Mr Hudson?' Libby

continued in the same professional but unemotional tone, only a little louder.

'Call me Maxwell. It's less formal,' he said with a smirk.

'Maxwell, as I said, please take a seat...' she motioned again to the chair '...and tell me what the problem appears to be.'

He sat down without taking his eyes off her. 'It's my back. I fell asleep in the sun and now I'm burnt.'

'I see. Please remove your shirt and I can take a look.'

Maxwell began unbuttoning his brightly coloured shirt, patterned with flamingos and palm trees. His eyes remained fixed on hers and he mimicked a male entertainer as he slowly undid each button, making Libby's discomfort grow by the second.

'I don't see a ring, pretty lady.'

Libby had a fairly good idea where the conversation was heading and she had no intention of helping it along. Quite the opposite, she was going to stop it dead in the water by ignoring it.

'It's such a lovely day and I'm sure you want to get back to the group so let's look at your sunburn.' Her tone was courteous and professional as she slipped on latex gloves.

She trusted she was making it clear she was not interested in his line of questioning.

'I'd rather stay in the cabin with you.'

Libby drew a deep breath. The man had the faint smell of whiskey and a strong smell of suntan lotion and bad cologne. The combined scents were as unpleasant as his personality. 'Well, I have a lot to do, so let's get you seen to and back out there.'

'It must be a bit dreary not being able to join the party,' he continued, still not following Libby's clear line of conversation.

'I'm on board to work. That's the only reason I'm here and I'm happy about that. Looking after Sir Walter will keep me busy enough.'

'When you finish your shift, you should come up on deck and get some sunshine with me.'

'I don't have a shift, I'm on call all the time. Now please turn around so I can look at the sunburn.'

'It's not that bad actually.' The man's mouth curled into a grin that immediately turned Libby's stomach. She had feared the worst and very quickly her fears were being realised.

'I came here to see you.'

'Then we're finished here.'

'Not so fast,' the man said. Standing up and moving closer, he grabbed her wrist with his stubby fingers. 'I watched you sitting by the pool yesterday with your girlfriend, in your skimpy shorts, and I did some digging around to find out about you. It seems you're single... and available.'

Libby tried to pull free but the man moved even closer. His breath was warm on her neck as he stared into her eyes. Suddenly, being in such close proximity to him, she noticed the stench of alcohol was not so faint.

'Let go of me now.' Her voice was raised and her tone cold as she pulled her arm free and moved to the other side of the room. A sense of panic was stirring inside. She was alone in the cabin with a drunken, lecherous man.

'Come on, don't play coy. The doctor's not here. It's just you and me. The rest of the group are up on deck, a long way from us, so let's make friendly.'

'Get away from me,' Libby yelled, trying to quell her anxiety. The situation had escalated from uncomfortable to dangerous very quickly. Her heart was picking up speed and she felt the heat rising from her core. Her fight-or-flight response was kicking in as she backed up to a wall-mounted telephone.

'Come on, you and I both know you signed up to have some fun. If you weren't the type to *party* you would've stayed on dry land,' he said as he reached for the zip on his shorts. 'And I'm the man who can give you a good time, right here, right now. I've got plenty of time to seal the deal.'

The door opened abruptly as the man reached for Libby. Seemingly unperturbed, he ignored the sound and continued to fumble with his shorts.

Daniel was standing in the doorway. With powerful strides he crossed the room, grabbed the man by the collar and spun him around. Libby could see the rage in Daniel's eyes. She had never seen him like that before. With her emotions on a roller-coaster, it both frightened and calmed her at the same time.

'Don't ever speak to a woman like that again,' Daniel roared. The volume and tone of voice commanded attention.

The man straightened up and looked Daniel up and down. Ignoring the uniform, he continued to display a level of arrogance that Libby found appalling.

'Chill out, buddy. Go back on duty and do your steward thing. It's all good…the little lady's happy to chat with me.'

'Nurse McDonald is most definitely not

happy to speak with you. She's made that clear. Now leave.' Daniel stood his ground and Libby felt very safe and protected by the man she had wanted to hate.

'Like I said, chill out. It's all good.'

'I said leave. Now.'

'Make me,' the now irate passenger said with a cocky expression on his alcohol-flushed face. He suddenly began shifting unsteadily from side to side on his feet as if he were in a boxing ring.

As Daniel stretched out his long arm to escort him outside, the man took a swing at him, his right hand clenched into a fist, trying to connect with Daniel's ribs.

'Daniel, be careful,' Libby called out with concern etching her voice. Concern for the man she had never wanted to see again in her life but was so relieved to see at that moment.

Daniel dodged the man's punch as it cut through the air. 'Don't be stupid,' Daniel told him. 'Just leave before you get hurt.'

'By who? You?' the passenger laughed scornfully as he tried yet again to punch Daniel but this time taking aim at his stomach.

Libby could see that Daniel had no choice but to act in self-defence. He deflected the man's punch with his forearm, then, grabbing the man's arm, twisted it behind his back and forced him to the floor in a secure hold, his knee resting firmly on the man's back.

'Please dial nine, Libby. It will put you through to the bridge. Ask the captain to send down the first mate and a steward to take care of this creep. I'm going to insist this excuse for a man is escorted off the ship when we arrive in port tomorrow morning.'

Without hesitation, Libby did as Daniel asked and explained the situation before turning back to see Maxwell restrained, red faced and unable to move as Daniel still had him pinned to the floor. Maxwell's eyes were darting about, his cheek pressed against the floor, and he was muttering inaudible comments to no one in particular. Perhaps his sober self was having regrets, she thought. She didn't care. He was a predator and she was relieved that Daniel was going to have him removed from the ship. Under the influence of alcohol or not, he was a risk that needed to be mitigated.

'You can't throw me off.'

'I can and I will,' Daniel said in a voice that continued to bring reassurance and calm to Libby. 'I'll speak with Walter immediately.'

'But I'm family,' Maxwell muttered. 'He won't throw me off. He'll throw you two off for treating me this way.'

'I don't think so, buddy. You're a risk to every woman on the ship and I'm not going to allow that risk to remain on board.'

The first mate and two stewards arrived within minutes to find Daniel still restraining Maxwell.

'There's always one who overdoes the alcohol and oversteps the mark,' the slightly taller of the well-built trio said. 'We can take it from here. I assume you'll be speaking with the captain or Sir Walter. This guy's probably family so it might be difficult to drop him off at the next port. If they keep him on board we'll just have him followed when he's out of his cabin.'

'I don't care who he is, he's getting off this vessel, no ifs, no buts about that. He's gone.'

Thwarted in his attempt to seduce Libby, and no doubt feeling humiliated by the ease with which Daniel had grappled him to the floor, the man had ceased struggling. He lay in a crumpled heap with Daniel clearly in control. But it was not lost on Libby that without Daniel it could have ended very differently.

It could have ended very badly.

As the door closed, leaving them alone, Daniel turned to Libby and looked at her for the longest moment before he spoke. His blue eyes were piercing her soul with the intensity of his gaze. It was as unnerving as it was comforting.

'Are you all right, Libby?' he finally asked in a voice that was strong and masculine but coloured with layers of warmth and tenderness.

His concern seemed genuine and his expression was serious but Libby could not answer for a moment. She was once again seeing Daniel and the man she had been so very close to, not the man she had wanted to forget. His eyes were drawing her in just as they had in the past. They were like two brilliant blue crystals but they were far from cold. And, against her will, their warmth was thawing her heart.

'I'm…fine,' she managed to say, with so many mixed emotions colouring every thought. His eyes looked so much like her precious son's that it caught her breath.

'I'm not so sure,' he replied and crossed the room, gently pulling her into his arms.

Libby wanted to fight him, she wanted to pull away but she couldn't. She fell into his embrace. Into the warmth of his chest and the strength of his arms around her. It was everything she needed at that moment. The past was gone and the future didn't matter. Libby just wanted to remain in the comfort of Daniel's arms for as long as she could.

There was a knock on the open door and they both turned to see Walter standing there with the chief stewardess beside him. Daniel dropped his arms and Libby stepped back, immediately creating space between them.

'I heard what happened, Libby,' Walter began. 'I'm so sorry, my dear. Are you all right?'

'I'm… I'm fine, thank you.' Her voice quavered from the reality of what had almost happened with Maxwell…and the embrace she had shared with Daniel.

'It appears you're fine because of our doctor.'

'Yes.' Libby nodded and looked fleetingly at Daniel. He was staring back at her, his concern for her evident in his expression. Her heart was torn with so many emotions. He had come to her rescue despite the way she had spoken to him the day before. Despite the way she had pushed him away.

'You're a strong woman, Libby,' Walter continued. 'I know that first hand but what you just faced is not something to brush off lightly. Maxwell is leaving the yacht tomorrow morning. The captain has called the coastguard and they're picking him up first thing and what they do with him, frankly, I don't care. For what he just did, I'd drop him in the middle of the ocean, to be honest, if I could get away with it. I've never liked him but he married his way into the family years ago and we've never been able to shake him. Well, we have now. And for good.'

'Thank you, Walter.'

'Don't thank me, Libby, thank Daniel. He was your knight in shining armour, rushing to your rescue, and it's a good thing he did,' Walter interjected. 'Now, you need to have a good rest in your cabin or on deck. You do not have to fuss over me for the rest of the day. I've told the steward to lock Maxwell in his cabin and if he tries to leave they can find a broom closet. I don't care where they damn well put him. They could strap him to a jet-ski for all I care.

'We'll let him sleep off the booze in preparation for his exit from the yacht, and the family, tomorrow. I'll be glad to see the back of him. He's been a leach for years but now he's crossed the line. I'm just so very sorry he stayed long enough to do this to you.'

'It wasn't your fault; no one could have known.'

'While that may be true, my dear, I'm going to try to make it up to you by having your belongings brought up to one of the empty suites on this deck.'

'There's no need, really.'

'Yes, there absolutely is a need,' Walter argued. 'That excuse for a man tried to assault you and would have succeeded if it wasn't for Daniel. The suite is adjacent to Daniel's and I think it might be reassuring for you to have him close by.'

With that, Walter and the chief stewardess left the cabin.

The suite next to Daniel's cabin? Libby wasn't sure that was such a good idea. For anyone.

'I'm truly sorry that happened…' Daniel began.

'You have nothing to apologise for,' Libby cut in, never having expected to say those words to him. 'I… I don't know what I would have done if you hadn't arrived.'

'Don't think about it, Libby. It's over and he's gone. For good, so you can relax for the rest of the journey knowing you don't have to look over your shoulder.'

Libby drew in a deep breath in an effort to still her nerves—about the attack and about being in the arms of her saviour. Both were playing on her mind.

'But how did you get here so quickly?' she asked with a curious expression on her face.

'I was just outside the cabin.'

'From when he arrived?'

'A minute or two afterwards,' Daniel told her, nodding his head and running his fingers through his hair. 'I know how you feel about me, Libby, and your determination not to spend time with me, and I don't blame you. I do understand. But I'd previously seen the jerk being incredibly disrespectful to the female crew members. He looked like potential trouble.

'I know the type too well. Too much sun and too much alcohol. I was going to raise the matter with Walter and the captain tonight but when I heard he was heading to see you with a medical condition I followed him and waited nearby. It's not that I don't trust in your ability to manage a situation as a nurse, Libby. Believe me, I've witnessed how you handle the most volatile situations in the ER but this was different. You were alone in a cabin and I feared it could go very wrong.'

Libby said nothing. Her anxiety was abating by the moment and, against her better judgement, her desire to once again be in

Daniel's strong arms was growing by the second.

'When you raised your voice, I knew that, despite your rules, I had no choice but to step in.'

Libby looked at him sheepishly and in a way she had not expected to ever again. He was not the man who had broken her heart, he was her handsome protector.

'I'm glad you did,' she said softly.

Daniel looked at her in silence for the longest time and she felt her heart melting. All the feelings she had buried were starting to resurface and she wasn't sure how to fight them. Or if she even wanted to try. The urge to feel his strong arms around her again was overwhelming. And unexpected. Libby suddenly saw Daniel for the man she had fallen in love with all those years ago. She was looking at the man who had captured her heart. And the way he was looking at her at that moment made her wonder if perhaps he had not forgotten what they had shared either. There were questions that needed answering…but did she want to know the answers now? They had a week to unpack the past. It was a silly way to think but her heart was leading her thoughts.

She was so confused at that moment. Adrenalin was still surging through her body, along with something else. A warm feeling. A feeling of safety. A feeling of something she couldn't define.

But she liked it and realised she'd missed that feeling.

And she'd missed him.

CHAPTER EIGHT

DANIEL STOOD LOOKING at Libby. He wanted her with every fibre of his being. He wanted to pull her back into his arms and carry her to his bed. He wanted to make love to her more than anything he had ever wanted. But he couldn't. It wasn't right for so many reasons. She was vulnerable. And he knew whatever they would share would only be for a few days. It couldn't be for ever. And Libby deserved better than that.

Libby deserved a forever man. And he could never be that. He had to step back. He had to walk away again but this time in the light of day and before he lost the ability to do it a second time.

'As long as you're okay, I should go,' Daniel said abruptly, pulling them both back to reality.

As he stepped away he fought the need to taste the sweetness of her mouth. It was a battle he had to win against his own desire for the woman so close to him he could smell the soft scent of her skin. He would recognise that scent anywhere. It was Libby's scent. It had been in his memory for the longest time.

But they could never be that close again.

No matter how much he wanted to be with Libby, Daniel knew he couldn't. That would be taking advantage of the situation. Taking advantage of her need to feel comforted after what she had just faced. Daniel knew that walking away all those years ago had been cruel but he believed his reasons had made it justified. Doing it again would be unforgivable.

He had to accept that being together wasn't in the stars for them. Fate had very different ideas for his future and he knew he cared for Libby too much to put her through what lay ahead for him. He wished with all his heart that the life ahead for him was a simple one that could include the most beautiful, kind, wonderful redhead he had ever met, but it couldn't.

His life would play out very differently from the one she deserved.

As he made his way to the door, he turned back to her. 'I'm sorry for what happened today, Libby. And, trust me, he will be gone in the morning. You'll never see his face again.'

Libby was taken aback. Daniel had just pushed her away. It was just as she had asked but that had been before she had fallen into his arms again. Before she had realised that she loved that feeling.

And wanted more.

Her heart sank a little. Her knight in shining armour was just passing through. Yet again. She felt so stupid for getting her hopes up and letting her heart be tempted, if only for a moment, toward the path that had broken it so completely all those years ago.

Biting the inside of her cheek, Libby watched Daniel leave the cabin and close the door behind him. And close the door on any chance for them, she told herself.

She would never be that stupid again. Clearly, she meant nothing to him or he would not have behaved so dismissively. He would not have walked away, leaving her standing there like a stranger he had rescued. Like any other colleague, not a woman who had fallen in love with him. Who had slept with him, no matter how long ago it might have been.

Libby couldn't help but wonder why the universe had brought Daniel back into her been the most wonderful evening, a fundraiser with an Easter theme. had been oversized glitter-covered floral arrangements on every one e hundred and fifty tables, and six-fed rabbits placed at the entrance in waistcoats and top hats. Daniel n a tuxedo as it had been a black-tie e women had worn glamorous floor-owns, adorned with jewels, some real e costume, and the men were a sea suits.

aniel had seen none of it once Libby ved. His breath had been taken away walked into the room wearing the nning white sequined gown. As she'd to greet another guest, his eyes had the bare curve of her back. Her red d been swept to one side and as she'd him staring at her, she'd smiled the eautiful smile back at him. Immedi-e'd realised she was not only the most us woman in the world, and without the most amazing nurse, she was dan-ly close to being the love of his life. l noticed they were seated on opposite of the same table so he had politely, and he other guests' approval, rearranged ating to be next to her. They'd chatted

life for only a few days. Perhaps it was to let her know he was not the right man for her. To remind her of what he had done and could do again.

To remind her that she was a strong woman, a mother and a nurse, and that was all she needed to be. She didn't need Daniel Dimosa and now she had five days to prove that to herself.

And to work out exactly what sort of man he really was. And if there would be a place in her son's life for him.

Daniel had no choice but to put distance between them. He was close to losing the ability to see reason and surrendering to his desire to pull Libby to him and tell her everything. Tell her that he hadn't wanted to leave her all those years ago. Tell her why he'd had to go but how much he wished he'd never left. But he couldn't do any of that so keeping her at bay was his only defence.

Sombrely he walked back to his cabin and shut the door. He needed to shut his heart on Libby. He went into the bathroom and washed his face with cold water. Staring into the mirror as he patted his skin dry with a hand towel, he knew he was in trouble. Libby McDonald was still in his heart and now she was within reach. And tonight she would be even closer. Her cabin would be right next to his. She would be lying in her bed with only a thin wall between them. A wall he would gladly break down, if only he could.

Stepping away from the mirror, he crossed to the open doors of his balcony. Looking out across the still blue water, all he could see was Libby's beautiful face.

He was struggling to understand why the world had brought them together, only to tear them apart.

That night, as he lay awake in his bed, Daniel thought back to the day he had first laid eyes on Libby at the Northern Bay General Hospital in San Francisco. With a short-term contract as head of ER, Daniel had instantly been taken by the beauty of the redheaded nurse who had efficiently organised everyone and everything in sight. As she'd rushed from one bay to the next, directing paramedics and nurses alike, he'd also seen the sweetness of her face and, as he'd drawn closer, the kindness in her eyes. The way she had engaged with the anxious patients and their loved ones was nothing quite like he had witnessed before.

The days had become weeks and as he'd

spent more time work… in ER, the more and … preciate her extraordi… She'd managed the yo… had been doing it for de… she was only in her late… sire to impart knowled… along the way to the y… medical students had … some days long after … She'd swept them up o… in the love she had for n…

Libby was born to hav… cine, he'd soon realised. … and, against his better jud… thing he had told himself … lived by, he'd soon felt hin… When they'd worked the sa… had pre-empted his needs … managed the most difficul… wonderful outcomes, othe… edy, but they had done it … never experienced before. … comfort to every situation. …

Daniel rolled over in bed … ceiling as his mind travelled … they had crossed the line. T… reached out for her not as a … a lover.

It had … a hospita… There h… eggs in … of the o… foot stu… dressed … had wo… affair. T… length g… and sor… of black…

But l… had arr… as she… most st… turned … roame… hair ha… caugh… most … ately, … gorge… doubt … gerou…

He … sides … with … the s…

all night about everything and anything. And then Daniel had asked her to dance.

It had been a dance like no other. As he'd taken Libby in his arms, her body had moulded to his, the softness of her perfume filling his senses. Her hair had brushed against his face and when she'd laughed and rested her head ever so lightly on his shoulder, he'd never wanted the night to end.

It had been after midnight when the band finished and their last dance had come to an end. Daniel had offered to drive Libby home and she'd accepted, with a smile that had lit up the room and his heart. When he'd walked her to the door, he leaned in to kiss her goodnight on the cheek but his lips had moved to find hers in the porchlight. Passion had overtaken them both and she'd invited him inside.

It had been the most wonderful night. He would never forget it but he would always regret it too. He should not have crossed the line.

With only a sheet covering his body, Daniel turned and stared out to sea. The curtains were open as they always were and the moonlight was dancing on the gently rolling black waves, painting them silver. Daniel had seen it many times before but tonight was different. Tonight he knew that Libby could be looking at the same darkened horizon from the window in the suite next to his.

The next morning, he woke with a resolve to keep his promise to himself and his family, no matter how difficult it might be. He was returning to Chezlovinka in four days. He could not complicate it further, neither would he ever hurt Libby again. There was a divide between them that he could never again cross. This time he could not afford to get swept up in his feelings.

Libby had finished breakfast when he arrived on deck, looking for her. He had taken a call from the chief stewardess when he'd stepped from the shower about a crew member who was unwell.

'Good morning, Libby.'

She turned and smiled a half-smile in his direction. 'Good morning, Daniel.'

He wanted to ask if she had slept well but decided to stay away from any personal conversation and keep it about work only. 'I hope you can put yesterday behind you. The coastguard picked up Maxwell early this morning.'

Libby nodded. 'Good to hear.' Her reply was without emotion and it made Daniel wonder what she might be thinking, but he knew he had no right to ask.

'If it's okay with you, we need to make a crew cabin call.'

'Why do you need me?' she asked curtly as she placed her plate back on the end of the buffet with others that had been used by guests.

'It's a young woman. She sounds a little distressed and is complaining of gastro symptoms. I hope to hell it's not, because we know that can spread through the ship very quickly. Her symptoms do sound vague but I'm also hoping it's not appendicitis. I would ordinarily go alone, as it's nothing I can't manage, but she asked for a female doctor. When we explained that wasn't possible, she asked for you to attend with me.'

'That's fine. Whatever she wants,' Libby replied matter-of-factly.

He suspected it was not her ideal situation, but she was showing him professional courtesy and he appreciated that.

'Thank you, Libby. I've got my bag with extra gloves, masks and a couple of disposable gowns just in case it is gastroenteritis,' he told her as he began walking in the direction of the glass elevator.

'If it is, how do you plan on controlling that on board?' Libby asked as she followed him.

'If I consider it a risk, I'll take away her swipe card and secure the cabin. If she has a cabin buddy we will keep an eye on them too and quarantine her in another cabin if possible. I don't like to do it but sometimes it's necessary even on a yacht this size. There's still four days' cruising to go and it would be unfair to the other passengers and particularly nasty for Walter.'

'Let me take that,' she said, reaching for the small bag. Her soft skin brushed against his as her fingers took the handle. His heart unexpectedly began racing as he had not been expecting her touch.

Libby suddenly released hold of the bag and stepped away from the elevator door. Neither made eye contact but each automatically created a distance between them. Daniel's reaction reaffirmed to him that it was going to be the most challenging four days of his life. He was still unsure how Libby felt but he realised it was best he didn't know.

They reached the cabin within a few minutes and Daniel checked his pager.

'The young woman's name is Alexandra and she just confirmed that she's been vomiting for two days now.'

Libby pulled from her bag the two disposable gowns, masks and a pair of gloves for each of them, which they immediately donned before knocking. Daniel had a swipe card that opened every one of the ship's cabins in case of an emergency.

'Come in,' a very drained and weary female voice called out.

Daniel and Libby stepped inside the tiny cabin with no windows. It was on the lowest deck and not too far from Libby's original cabin. Alexandra, still dressed in pink pyjamas, was sitting on a chair with her head resting in her hands. Her complexion was drained of any hint of colour.

'Hello, I'm Dr Dimosa and this is Nurse McDonald but please call us Daniel and Libby,' Daniel said, then looked at Libby for approval.

It was after the fact, but Libby nodded her agreement; she was happy to use her less formal first name and with what they were facing she wasn't overly fussed whatever they called her.

'I'm Alex,' the woman said in a strained voice and little energy behind her words. 'I've seen you both around but I didn't know what you did. I'm a cleaner. I do some galley work now and then but mainly clean the suites.'

'Please tell us what's happening and how you're feeling now,' Daniel said.

'I've been throwing up for two days and I'm not sure if it's something I ate or sea sickness but whatever it is I feel dreadful.'

'When did this start? And what were your initial symptoms?' Daniel continued, as he reached back to find Libby was already holding the digital thermometer he wanted. He couldn't help but smile to himself. Naturally she had known what he would be needing next; she always had.

'It was about two days ago, when I woke up. I thought it was something I ate because I felt a bit queasy,' the woman began.

Daniel rested the thermometer gently inside the woman's ear and it quickly beeped the reading. 'Thirty-six point five,' he reported to Libby, who was already taking notes. 'You don't have a temperature. Not even a low-grade fever.'

'Is that good? What does it mean?'

'It means your body's not fighting a bacterium or virus so there must be another reason for the nausea,' he said as he turned to find Libby reaching for the thermometer, discarding the disposable cap, wiping the handle clean with antibacterial wipes and returning it to the medical bag. She was her ever efficient self.

'But what can you give me to make it stop? I've been vomiting for hours and my stomach hurts,' the woman asked. 'And I want to get back to work.'

'Before I give you anything, I would like to know what we are dealing with.'

'I feel like death warmed up again, but...' she paused as she made her way to the bunk and lay down, pulling the covers up to her chin protectively '...it did improve both days after lunch.'

'So the nausea stopped completely after lunchtime?'

'Yes, I had some dry toast and then by dinnertime I was fine and then it started again the next morning. Last night I was fine again and I ate a good dinner and could work but now today it's back,' she said with her eyes starting to close. 'I'm exhausted with all of this throwing up. Is it seasickness? I've never worked on a boat before.'

'No, Alexandra, I don't think so.'

'Then what is it?' she mumbled wearily, her blue eyes as pale and drawn as her skin.

'Your lack of fever and the transient nausea are leading me to believe it might be a case of morning sickness...'

'Morning sickness?' The young woman almost yelled her response as she sat bolt upright. 'Are you telling me I'm pregnant?'

Libby silently agreed with Daniel's diagnosis. While it wasn't how she had felt when she'd been pregnant, it was a common symptom during the first trimester of pregnancy. For her entire pregnancy she had been overtaken by cravings for food she couldn't ordinarily stomach and, once she had given birth, never ate again.

'I'm putting it forward as a possibility,' he said calmly. 'We would need to confirm with a pregnancy test and then bloodwork.'

'I can't be pregnant. It's not possible,' she said, shaking her head as she slumped back against the pillows.

'You haven't had sex in the last month?'

Alexandra looked down at her hands, they were trembling slightly in her lap.

'Or months,' Daniel added. 'If you are pregnant, you may have conceived a few months ago and be further along in the pregnancy.'

'This is a mess,' she said, turning back to face Daniel and Libby with tears welling in her eyes. 'I haven't had a period in over eight weeks but I thought it was the stress of the separation. I left my husband six weeks ago.'

'I'm sorry,' Daniel and Libby said simultaneously.

Libby leaned in and instinctively put her arm around the young woman to comfort her.

'We were told we couldn't have children naturally—' Alexandra continued.

'Again,' Daniel cut in as he looked at the woman with compassion, 'I'm not saying that you are pregnant but it's something we need to consider as the symptoms do align.'

'I can't believe it,' she returned, as she began shaking her head again. 'If it's true, the timing couldn't be worse. I just secured the job with Sir Walter and I really need to keep it. I'm employed to clean the yacht when he cruises and look after his house in Miami the rest of the time. He's a good boss and I need the money to pay rent now that I'm not living with my husband.'

Daniel nodded. 'Walter is a good man, Alex, and I can have a word with him once we know if you're pregnant and see what sort of arrangement can be made for maternity leave. Do you have any other support at home?'

Libby pulled her arm away slowly and turned her attention to the medical bag nearby. She wondered if there was a pregnancy test inside. It was a long shot but if there was one on board it would either confirm or negate the pregnancy diagnosis and ensure any decisions made by Alexandra were based on fact.

'No, my mother and father passed away in an accident in Mexico three years ago. It was just my husband and me and now…now it's just me.'

Libby was surprised to find a two-window pregnancy test. While it was what she wanted, it wasn't what was normally in a medical bag—but, then, she surmised that a medical bag on a cruise ship was not a regular medical bag. She checked the date then held it up for Daniel, her eyes signalling her intention to suggest Alex take the test. He nodded his response.

'There's a pregnancy test here,' Libby announced in a low and equally calm voice. 'Would you like to go to the bathroom and find out one way or another? As Daniel said, you'll need bloods when you return to shore but these over-the-counter pregnancy tests become more accurate all the time.'

'How does it work?'

'It will detect the hormone chorionic gonadotropin. When an egg's fertilised and attaches to your uterine wall, the placenta begins to form and produces this hormone, and it appears in your bloodstream and your urine. As you get further along in pregnancy, the hormone levels rise more rapidly, doubling every couple of days. That's why if the test is positive, you'll need to see your obstetrician in the next week or so to gauge how far along you are in your pregnancy.'

The young woman reached in silence to take the test kit from Libby and then swung her feet around and slowly moved to stand up. She was still visibly weak so Libby held her arm as she made her way to the bathroom.

'Do you know what to do?' Libby asked. 'It's a two-window test so two lines indicate positive and a single line is negative. But, remember, while the positive result is generally accurate, the negative may not be definite and if the symptoms continue you may want to visit your GP for bloodwork.'

'I've done this too many times before and each time it's been negative and that never changed with a blood test,' she said as she stepped inside the tiny bathroom.

'We're nearby, if you need us,' Libby said without making any further comment as she closed the bathroom door.

Libby was distracted thinking about the anxiety surging through Alex behind the small bathroom door. She knew and understood it first-hand. For Libby it was a lived experience, and one she would never forget. She reached for her locket and held it in her gloved hand, wondering if in the not-too-distant future Alex would be holding a much-loved child in her arms.

She looked over at Daniel and felt a pang of guilt. He had no idea what she'd been through on her own. Part of her was still angry and part of her felt sad for him that he had not been able to share the joy of the little boy who was his son.

If he had known, perhaps he still would have stayed away. Perhaps he would have returned, not for her but for his son.

'If she's pregnant,' Daniel suddenly said, breaking her thoughts and completely unaware of the enormous decision weighing heavily on her mind, 'Alexandra's nausea might be temporary with any luck, and she might be a mother-to-be who has cravings more than sickness. My mother was apparently like that when she was pregnant with me. Lived on olives, grilled fish and home-made bread for months.'

Libby's eyes grew wide. She couldn't believe what Daniel was telling her. He was describing exactly her pregnancy diet with Billy.

The door opened tentatively and Alex stood

there crying, her body visibly shaking, with the test in her hand.

'There are two lines. I'm pregnant. I'm actually going to be a mother,' she said through tears. 'I'm so happy and so sad and so confused. It's all I ever wanted and now I'm not sure I can do it. Not alone.'

Libby, still reeling a little from Daniel's story, crossed to Alexandra and took her arm to lead her back to the chair. 'Sit down and catch your breath. It's a lot to take in. Particularly when it's unexpected.'

'I'm… I'm happy. I'm actually so happy but I'm not sure what to do. It's all so surreal to me and part of me still can't believe it. We went through three rounds of IVF and three negative pregnancy tests and my husband said he couldn't go through it again.

'It wasn't just the cost. The devastation of the last negative test made me go a little crazy. I wanted a baby so much and my husband shut the door on the idea. He said the hormones I had to take made me so sick and he didn't want me to go through that again. He said he loved me too much to do that but his decision ripped us apart. I wanted to try just one more time. I knew he would be the best father and we would be so happy. With no parents, a family of our own meant the world to me. But he wouldn't. He said it wasn't meant to be.'

'I understand, and I might be out of line here,' Libby began, 'but your husband sounds like a very caring man who made that decision from concern for you.'

'I know. I still love him, I always will, but…we did nothing but argue and then I went into my shell and shut him out because I wanted a baby so badly.'

'And now that's become a reality,' Daniel said, rubbing his chin. 'While it's unexpected, I'd say it's a great outcome.'

'But what if I lose the baby? What would happen? I would go completely crazy and I can't put him through that,' she said as she moved to the bed and curled up into a foetal position, pulling the covers over her. 'I can't do that to him, I can't.'

'It looks like we're both at risk of being out of line,' Daniel started, 'but I think you might be selling your husband short on this one. There's no indication that you'll miscarry, so if you don't tell your husband he will have missed the joy of these months. The joy of finding out he's going to be a father. That would be a very special time for him. Don't take that away from him. My advice, both professionally and as a man, would be to let him know.'

'But what if something goes wrong with the pregnancy?'

'You're jumping to the worst-case scenario,' Daniel said as he drew closer and looked intently at Alexandra. 'As I said, unless the obstetrician has identified an issue and told you there would be a risk, you should not be overly concerned. You're young and appear otherwise healthy so make sure you see your GP and obstetrician and start an antenatal plan, and seriously take this time to consider bringing your husband up to speed with the fact he's going to be a father. Give him the chance to step up. I'm not a counsellor, but you said you still love him so at least give him the chance to tell you and your baby the same thing.'

Libby felt a lump rising in her throat with every word that slipped from Daniel's lips. The previous pang of guilt threatened to become a tsunami of regret.

Her mind was spinning and her stomach churning in a way they never had before.

She and Alex each had a huge decision to make.

But Libby had only five more days before the opportunity might be gone for ever.

CHAPTER NINE

LIBBY SPENT THE following days concentrating on Walter. He didn't like any fuss, so she caught up with him after he had enjoyed his breakfast on the deck, after lunch and then just before he retired to his luxurious cabin for the night, checking his blood pressure and his wound. Despite the less than healthy diet, her patient was progressing very well. The wound was healing nicely and his blood pressure was back within normal limits. The sea air certainly agreed with him.

When she wasn't with Walter, she returned to the quiet of her suite to call home and check in with Billy and her parents—and more importantly avoid seeing Daniel. She had done some soul searching after hearing Daniel speak openly and honestly to Alex about her need to tell her husband about her pregnancy. It wasn't a decision she was making in haste, the way she had done the night

Daniel had driven her home. She was going to tell Daniel that he had a son.

Her decision was born from thinking hard about the words Daniel had imparted to Alex, both as a doctor and as a man, and knowing in her heart they were true. Libby didn't want to keep Daniel from his son to punish him. With hand on heart, she knew her immediate reaction had been to protect Billy but she had to trust that in letting Daniel know, whatever the outcome she had not prevented Billy from having the opportunity to know his father.

Now it would be up to Daniel whether he wanted to take on that role. And what that role in Billy's life might look like in the coming years.

The time alone in her cabin was giving Libby the space she needed to think about everything.

She could not be sure that Daniel would not leave Billy the way he had left her four years ago, without an explanation and with no way to contact him, but it was a chance she had to take. She just had to get the timing right. If he reacted badly and they still had a few days at sea, it would not be fair on Walter and the rest of the passengers. Libby decided she would tell him the night before they docked. It would give her sufficient time to tell him everything, answer his questions, and then he could process his feelings about it alone, not trapped on the yacht surrounded by a group of strangers.

Libby had no reason to socialise too much. Georgie was busy with preparations for the upcoming engagement party and the day-to-day running of the galley. It was busier than she had thought so they both caught up every evening for half an hour to chat and then head to bed early. That was the time when Libby called home because there was a time difference.

She missed Billy, Bradley and her parents. She had no intention of raising the fact that Daniel was on the yacht to either Bradley or her parents as she didn't want to be swayed by their bias. They would naturally want to protect both her and Billy and none of them had known Daniel. Not the man she'd fallen in love with, at least. They had only known him as the cad who had broken her heart. So their opinion no doubt would not favour Daniel.

Libby headed down to see Walter on the morning they docked at Martinique. She needed to know if Walter intended to go ashore with his guests. If so, she would accompany him; if not, she would remain on the yacht and head to her cabin until his next medical check was due.

'Are you heading to the island today, Walter?'

'I've done it more times than I care to count,' he told Libby as she packed away the blood pressure monitor and stethoscope and sat down beside him. 'And between you and me, I could do with some peace and quiet with that lot gone for a few hours.'

Libby smiled, happy that she could just relax.

'How's my ticker doing anyway?' he asked. 'Is sacrificing my whisky and cigars paying dividends?'

'Absolutely. Your blood pressure is perfect and your scar is healing so well you'll hardly notice it when you're sunbathing on your next cruise.'

'My next cruise will be without those monkeys,' Walter scoffed as he looked in the direction of the guests disembarking the yacht. 'The extended family on Contessa's side are the worst. They're noisy, obnoxious and for the most part quite ungrateful...not to mention the clothing. I loved my wife; she was a beautiful, stylish woman, not unlike Grace Kelly, but her family are quite a different matter altogether. They have the most terrible dress sense. Abominable is more to the point. I know she wasn't adopted but I've always wondered where she fitted in. It's fortunate that I met Contessa first; if I'd met them I might have run in another direction.'

Libby bit the inside of her cheek so she didn't laugh as she watched the dozen or so family members heading ashore. She had to agree that their clothing was very loud and there were myriad patterns with a Hawaiian feel to them. She could only imagine what Bradley would have said.

'I do love my side of the family, of course,' he continued. 'My brother and his wife passed away a few years back now but they had the most gorgeous daughter, Sophia. She is the image of her mother and since Contessa and I were not blessed with children of our own, we unofficially adopted her when she was seventeen and she came to live with us for a little while until she went to college.

'As I said, she is the most perfect creature ever created and I love to spoil her whenever I can, which is why I'm throwing her this party. She's all grown up now—twenty-nine and an investment banker. She looks more like a model but she has a heart of gold and a mind like a steel trap. I think that's why we get on so well.'

'You modelled too?' Libby asked with a cheeky smile.

'I like you. You're funny. My side of the family will like you too; they're all flying in to San Lucia tomorrow. Should be a splendid night and I'm so excited to be seeing Sophia again. She did visit me in hospital but it was a whirlwind trip on her way to France to meet her fiancé's parents.'

'I'm sure she'll be excited to see you too.'

'You're very kind, Libby,' he said with a smile as he reached for his freshly squeezed juice. 'Tell me about your family. Do you have any shockers like the ones who just headed off to scare the locals?'

Libby laughed. 'My family is a little quieter. I adore them and I'm their only child,' she said, and without thinking she reached for her locket and held it in her hand as she spoke. 'My mother and father live quite close to my home in a suburb in San Francisco.'

'I think being close to your parents is lovely. It doesn't happen much nowadays. Everyone is on the go and travelling all over the world for work, never in one place for too long.'

'My parents are both retired and rarely travel, and being a single mother it's wonderful having them there to help out...' Libby stopped in mid-sentence. She hadn't meant the words to slip out and wished she could take them back. She'd been so careful not to mention Billy for five days and now she had just told him everything. Well, almost everything.

'Oh, you're a mother?'

She shifted in her seat uncomfortably but knew it was too late. Trying to hide the fact would only make it worse. 'Yes, I have a son.'

'Tell me more. How old is he and what's his name?'

'Billy…he's just turned three,' she managed to tell him, all the while wishing she had never opened up about her personal life.

'Just turned three… Hey, when was his birthday?'

'Last week, on the tenth of January.'

'That's three days after my birthday. He must be a lovely little chap.' He chuckled, then leaning in he whispered, 'You know, I was told by my mother that I was an Easter Bunny surprise. Of course, I worked out as I grew up that meant I was the result of a night of lovemaking in April after perhaps too many chocolates and champagne for my mother and more than likely a Guinness or two for my father.'

Libby froze. She couldn't laugh along with

Walter. She swallowed as she remembered the Easter fundraiser the night Daniel had driven her home. There had been no chocolates or Guinness but there had definitely been a night of lovemaking that April. She felt heat rushing to her cheeks. She had tried to push the night from her memory but now it was coming back to her at lightning speed.

'It's lovely to know a little more about you, Libby,' he said, putting the glass down again, to her relief completely unaware of her reaction to the conversation. He reached for a scone. 'But I'm going to cut our chat short because you are too young to stay on board with an old man who you just confirmed is as fit as a Mallee bull…'

'A Mallee bull?' Libby asked with a quizzical look. Her mind was spinning with what she had confessed and now they were talking about bulls.

'It's Australian slang for healthy. Comes from the Mallee region in Victoria, where there are a lot of cattle and where I invested in a sheep station. They can be an odd bunch in the land Down Under, and they use funny terms like that. I've picked up one or two on my travels there.'

'I never heard it before. I've learned something today.'

'And you'll learn more by heading ashore and exploring the island. Georgie told me you haven't travelled much so don't waste this time sitting with me when you can enjoy life in the Caribbean.'

Libby was still trying to calm her nerves. She had never expected their conversation to be so revealing. It was unexpected and she hoped it would not complicate her plans to tell Daniel about Billy in a few days. 'Thank you, Walter, but I'm very happy to stay on board today.'

'Hogwash,' he retorted. 'I've arranged company for you for the day, so there's no point arguing.'

'You've asked Georgie to go with me?'

'No, my dear,' Walter replied. 'She's up to her neck making an engagement cake for tomorrow night's party, so I asked Daniel. He was quick off the mark to accept the invitation and he should be here any minute.'

Libby suddenly felt her heart pick up speed. She had hoped to avoid Daniel for the next few days until she was ready to confess everything.

'Goodness, you suddenly look flushed, my dear. Let me pour you a glass of water,' Walter said as he reached for the pitcher of chilled water and filled a glass. 'Take this.'

Libby accepted the glass and drank the water quickly. 'Thank you. I'm sorry about that. I don't think I had enough fluids today,' she lied. She had no choice. She could not tell Walter that the thought of spending the day with Daniel was not what she wanted or needed.

'Make sure you take a bottle of water with you today, young lady. Can't have my nurse unwell on the island. Daniel might have to carry you back on board,' he said with a laugh.

Libby heard footsteps and turned her head slowly to see Daniel approaching from the other end of the deck. He was wearing a white T-shirt and beige shorts. His tanned feet were slipped inside dark-coloured espadrilles and he had a baseball cap covering his hair. He was dressed for a day on the island. And he looked so very handsome. Just as she knew Billy would one day.

Libby quickly climbed to her feet. She needed a few moments to calm her nerves. Her thoughts were racing and she felt emotionally dishevelled. Time alone together was definitely not in her plans.

'I'll go and change into something more suitable,' she told Walter, unsure of exactly what she intended to do but she knew if she could find an excuse not to go, she would. 'Please let Daniel know I'll be back as soon as I can.'

With that, Libby made her way to the glass elevator without passing Daniel. Ordinarily she would take the spiral staircase to the next deck but that would mean crossing paths with him.

As she stood waiting for the glass doors to open, she heard Walter call out cheerily, 'Good morning, Daniel. I can see you're all ready for your island date with Libby.'

Libby's hand began shaking as she pressed the call button again. *A date?* Was that just Walter's perception or was there any possibility that Daniel saw it that way too? She wished more than ever that she had never accepted the assignment to care for Walter. She would never have seen Daniel again and her life would not once again have been turned upside down by him. Her emotions were firmly strapped in on the roller-coaster and she couldn't escape.

The doors opened and she stepped inside and turned to see Daniel looking in her direction. Her heart began racing again. While she intended to go through with her decision to tell him about Billy, she was growing more concerned by the minute that her feelings for him were unfortunately still very real. The way her heart skipped a beat when his hand accidentally brushed against hers, how she'd felt so safe in his arms after the horrible situation with Maxwell, and finally seeing him appear on the deck ready for their *date*.

All of it was telling her that she was at risk of losing her heart to the man again if she didn't take control of her feelings and the reality of the situation. Her focus had to be on letting Daniel know about Billy in the right way and at the right time, and establishing a relationship with him that would allow him to be in Billy's life if he chose to do so. Full stop. Nothing more. Nothing romantic. No risk to her heart. None at all.

Trying her best to keep everything in perspective and on the task at hand, Libby changed into something more suitable for sightseeing. She chose a floral summer dress that skimmed her knees and flat white sandals. With a straw hat in her hand and a cross-body purse holding the few things she would need, she made her way to the door, knowing the day ahead would be challenging but an important part of telling him about Billy.

As she descended the highly polished oak staircase to the deck again, she decided the time she would be spending on the island with Daniel was purely an opportunity to find out more about him. Perhaps he had changed. Her stomach churned a little; she couldn't deny she was worried that he would raise the topic of their past and that it would hurt her to hear the truth. Or perhaps he would keep everything close to his chest and still stand behind the only explanation she had heard so far: *it was complicated.*

Had it just been a one-night stand that she had mistaken for more? Had Daniel been planning on leaving the hospital anyway and had assumed she knew? There were so many questions but she wasn't going there. The day was all about Billy. Libby needed to know enough about Daniel to know she was right in her decision to open up her life and that of her son to the man who had broken her heart. She had to make sure, as best she could, that he wouldn't break Billy's heart too.

'Ahh, there you are,' Walter said with a smile as Libby drew closer. 'You were quicker changing than my wife ever was. Must be the nurse in you. Always efficient and, I must say, looking very pretty.'

'Thank you, Walter,' Libby replied, not looking in Daniel's direction.

'I agree,' Daniel said, thinking that she looked far more than just pretty. He thought she looked stunningly beautiful. Just as she always had. Just as he had remembered her over the years.

'Then off you two go. Make the most of this beautiful weather and don't worry about me. You have your pager and I have the captain, the chief stewardess and a whole crew, so I'm well covered. And as a bonus I have a day of peace without those blessed, noisy folk who drive me to drink!'

Daniel nodded and Libby smiled a half-smile before they turned and made their way to the gangway. Libby held on tightly to the railing and Daniel suspected the rocking of the yacht in the shallower water made her a little nervous of falling into the marina. She didn't have to worry, he thought. He would be there to catch her for the next few days. In fact, if the world had been a different place, and he'd had any control of the future, he would always be there to catch her...in his arms.

'What would you like to do, Libby, shopping, sightseeing or an early lunch?'

Libby looked at her watch. 'Lunch sounds lovely.'

Daniel looked around. It wasn't his first

time on the island and he had a favourite street market he wanted to show Libby that wasn't too far away so they could be back if there was any emergency on the yacht.

'This way,' he said, and began walking past the street vendors selling fresh fish and produce. He watched as Libby looked around, her eyes wide as she took in the sights and smells of the colourful French Caribbean island. 'It's not too far.'

It took all of Daniel's self-control not to reach for her and pull her close as they walked. He wished he could hold her hand and as lovers visit the island together for the first time. But he could not behave the way his heart was wanting. He had to allow his head to control every part of his behaviour. He just wanted to spend time with Libby and hopefully heal the hurt he had inflicted, although he wasn't sure how he could do that.

It didn't take long for them to reach the bustling street market.

'Martinique is a French Caribbean island so the food is French with a Caribbean twist,' Daniel told her as they made their way to a stall where he could see the food he loved and hoped that Libby would also enjoy.

'What exactly does that mean? I've not

eaten much French food and I have no idea what Caribbean cuisine would be like.'

'The two most popular dishes are Boudin Creole and Boudin Blanc. I think you'd like the Boudin Blanc. The Creole is made from pork, pig's blood, onion and other ingredients…' Daniel paused as he noticed Libby's nose wrinkling up as he spoke. 'Just as I thought. Blanc it is.'

'What's in the second one?' she asked, her face not masking her concern.

'It's a white sausage made from pork, without the blood, and includes prawns, crabs, sea snail or fish.'

'That sounds much nicer.'

Daniel ordered two portions of the Boudin Blanc in his best French and then stepped back to Libby.

'I didn't know you spoke French.'

'I suppose there was no need to use it when…' He paused, feeling awkward about how to frame that time. He'd wanted to say *when I fell for you*, but he knew he couldn't tread that path.

'When we worked together,' Libby cut in, to his relief, and then continued, 'I guess not. San Francisco probably doesn't have a large French population.'

The brightly dressed woman behind the

counter called Daniel's name and he stepped up and collected two plates of food and they made their way to a table for two nearby. The chairs didn't match and the table was faded by the sun but he noticed that Libby didn't seem taken aback by it. Daniel sat the plates down and then pulled out her chair for her. She immediately leaned down towards the plate in front of her.

'It smells delicious.'

'It is, believe me,' he said. 'I'll just get us some drinks. What would you like?'

'Water would be lovely, if it's okay to drink the water on the island.'

'I'll get bottled water for you.'

Daniel bought two bottles of water and returned to find Libby looking around her. The sun was dancing on the red waves of her hair and kissing her bare shoulders the way he remembered. While he loved being with Libby, there was an ache in his heart for what he could not have.

After their lunch Daniel suggested a walk by the shore.

'That sounds lovely,' Libby told him as they left their table and began walking down towards the beach.

Their conversation was light and mostly about the island.

'You seem to know a lot about Martinique. It's very beautiful and serene,' Libby said as she looked out across the creamy white sand to the still, blue water.

'For the most part it's a very pretty island...'

'For the most part?' She repeated his words with a questioning inflection as she slipped her sandals off and walked barefoot on the soft sand.

'Like most places in the world today, there is a risk at times. It wouldn't be advisable to wander around the largely empty back streets of Fort-de-France after dark. It's an area best left alone after the sun sets.'

Libby nodded and continued looking around. 'The names of the places and the food just roll off your tongue. How many times exactly have you visited?' she asked as they walked a little further.

'I can't be sure. I've lost count over the years, to be honest, but I do love it. I've worked on the cruise ships that call in at Martinique with tourists for the last few years.'

Libby looked at him then looked away back out to sea. 'I'm sure you've seen many exotic places.'

'Yes, I've travelled all over the world. I've been the ship's doctor on trips through the

Caribbean, the Bahamas, Alaska and even all the way over to Australia and New Zealand.'

Daniel noticed Libby's mood suddenly shift and she fell silent, appearing to be deep in thought. She looked up towards the cloudless sky then walked away towards the shade of a huge palm tree.

'That must have been a culture shock from ER in a major hospital?' Libby said as she sat down, smoothing her dress out on the sand and crossing her ankles. 'I mean, one day you're in an inner-city emergency room and the next you're travelling the world on a yacht or cruise liner.'

One day in your bed and the next on a plane to the other side of the country, Daniel thought. He suspected the question was not just about the culture shock but more about the shock of his hasty departure.

'Libby,' he began as he sat down beside her, 'everything about the time with you in San Francisco was unexpected. You have to believe me, I didn't plan for any of it to happen and I wanted to explain everything to you but as I told you before, my life is complicated.'

'Perhaps we should leave that alone, Daniel,' she cut in without turning to face him. 'But I do want you to know that I would never have slept with you if I thought it was going

to be a casual one-night stand and that you'd
be gone before the sun came up. That's not
who I am.'

'It wasn't just a casual one-night stand.'

Libby looked out across the water, saying
nothing.

'It meant so much more to me than that,'
he told her.

'Let's not go there, Daniel. I really don't
want to spend the day talking about the past,'
she said, turning to face him. 'That was not
my intention. We need to make peace with
whatever it was that happened between us.'

'Libby, believe me when I say that I'm truly
sorry I caused you pain. I swear that if I could
take it back I would.'

'Which part, sleeping with me or leaving
in the middle of the night?'

'Leaving,' he told her honestly, not sure if
she had heard him. 'Until my dying day I will
never regret making love to you.'

CHAPTER TEN

LIBBY WOKE UP THE next day remembering Daniel's words but not knowing whether to believe them.

'Until my dying day I will never regret making love to you, Libby.'

Goddamn it, why did he have to say that?

None of it made sense to her and now he was making her life even more complicated. Whatever he said, it didn't change anything. His life was apparently *complicated*.

Well, life *was* complicated, for so many people, including her. Daniel didn't have the monopoly on a complicated life.

And he had no clue just how complicated hers had become because of him.

They had returned to the yacht without saying anything else to each other. She had to find the right time to tell Daniel about Billy and at the same time ensure she set ground rules. Billy deserved that. She wished her son had a daddy who would kiss him goodnight every evening and hug him every morning. While Daniel clearly couldn't be that man, she hoped he would find a way to be a part of Billy's life. Not be someone who might show up every few years or who Billy might bump into occasionally on an exotic island in the Caribbean.

There was a hurried knock on the door and Libby jumped out of bed, threw on her robe and rushed to open it.

Georgie was standing there with a look of panic on her face. 'I'm so sorry to bother you this early but Alexandra's throwing up again and I can't have her near the food, particularly not the engagement cake.'

'Come in,' Libby said, opening the door wider. 'Of course, it's the engagement party tonight. I'll help you in any way I can. I just need to check on Walter...'

'Daniel's already doing that,' Georgie cut in as she closed the door. 'He said he'll look after Walter, get him dressed and to the party on time. The other guests can make their own way there and the lovebirds flew in last night. They're staying at the resort already with the rest of the UK guests who also flew in late yesterday. The party is on the beach near the resort and the event planner arrived two days ago and has a local team already setting up before we dock.'

Libby curled her unruly bed hair into a makeshift bun and reached for a hair tie on the nearby table to keep it in place. 'It sounds like it's all organised, a bit like a military exercise. Let me know what you need and I'm there.'

Georgie gave her the biggest hug. 'I knew I could count on you.'

'Always.'

'Okay, we dock in San Lucia in a few hours so perhaps have your shower, get ready and pack a dress for the party...'

'I'm not going to the party,' Libby corrected her friend. 'I'm going to help you so I can wear shorts and a T-shirt because I'll be out of sight.'

'That's just it. I only need you to help me with some dessert preparation in the galley as I'm such an annoying perfectionist and I have to have someone I trust to manage quality control. Alexandra is as fussy as me but, as I said, unfortunately she's out of the picture, so you're my go-to. I'll also need you to help me put the cake together when we get to the party. It's baked and decorated but I have to assemble it on the beach.'

'We can't do that on the yacht?'

Georgie laughed. 'Can you imagine what could go wrong carrying a five-tier cake across the sand?'

'Five tiers? How many guests are coming?'

'I think close to a hundred and fifty. Some are sailing in and others have flown in. It's quite the social event. There are whispers that a couple of Hollywood A-listers will be there too.'

'Goodness, it sounds like all the more reason for me to stay in the background and look after the last-minute bits and pieces for you.'

Georgie appeared to ignore Libby's remark and, making her way to the closet, she opened the doors where there were only uniforms. 'Where are all your clothes?'

'In my suitcase,' Libby replied matter-of-factly.

'But you have a huge space in this stateroom. Why on earth are you not using it?'

'Because I wear my uniform most days and the rest of my clothes I can pull out of my suitcase and throw on.'

'Do you have *anything* glamorous in said suitcase?'

'Glamorous? But it's an island party. Wouldn't shorts or a cotton dress be okay?'

Georgie shook her head. 'No, they wouldn't. There will be the most fabulously dressed people at the party and you are absolutely not going to look like Orphan Annie. You, my friend, have to look equally fabulous.'

Libby suddenly thought Georgie sounded decidedly like Bradley.

'Where's your suitcase?' Georgie asked as she looked around the room.

Libby pointed to the second closet on the other side of the dressing table. 'It's in that one.'

Without wasting a second, Georgie sprang into action, crossed the room and found the suitcase lying inside the closet. She dragged it out onto the carpeted floor, opened it and began looking through the clothes like a woman on a mission. Within seconds she came upon the emerald-green silk dress. 'This,' she announced, climbing to her feet with the dress in her hands like a triumphant explorer with a golden chalice, 'is perfect. Just perfect. Do you have any shoes?'

'There are some gold strappy sandals in there somewhere but honestly, Georgie, please just let me help out in the kitchen and leave the party to the guests. I won't know anyone anyway.'

Georgie ignored Libby's pleas and continued to rummage around until she found the gold shoes in a plastic bag at the bottom of the suitcase. She unzipped the bag and held them up. 'Gorgeous. Not too high for navigating the walkways that are being erected on the sand leading to the floating pontoon.'

'A floating pontoon?'

'Yes, a floating pontoon with a Caribbean band. I'm not sure if you're aware that Walter is one of the wealthiest men in the UK, if not the world and he doesn't do things by halves—neither does his niece Sophia, I've heard. That's why I have to get this cake to be just perfect and you will be responsible for ensuring no one, and I mean no one, including those strange family members sharing the yacht with us, goes near the cake before the lovebirds cut it. I don't want anyone hovering too close and being tempted to touch it. That's why you must be dressed up and looking your gorgeous self so you can blend in and still be on cake duty.

'There was a strict direction from the event planner that they did not want anyone snapped in photos not looking the part. Alexandra even brought a lovely dress with her but I can't risk her throwing up at the party. Can you imagine Walter's reaction to that? Not to mention the guests having a fit and jumping into the water to get away. Now, that would make the front page of the tabloids!'

Libby could see Georgie's point and agreed to help her friend out. 'Okay, I'll pack my things into…actually, I don't know what to pack them in but I'll find something and then I'll jump in the shower, get dressed and head down to the galley to help you.'

'You're the best friend ever,' Georgie said, hugging Libby again and then making her way to the door. 'Don't rush. We don't dock for a few hours so there's plenty of time to do the prep work on the desserts. And you will be my pseudo apprentice sous chef.'

Libby thought that sounded outside her skill set but she could definitely manage some simple prep work in the galley and guard the cake, but that was her limit. She had only been cooking for Billy and herself for the last few years so her repertoire consisted of simple healthy food with lots of vitamins but no fancy plating. She hoped Georgie wasn't going to expect too much.

About thirty minutes later there was another knock on the door and Libby, still dressed in a towel and drying the mop of her hair, rushed to open it. 'I won't be long, Georgie—' she began, and then, lifting her head, realised it wasn't Georgie. It was Daniel standing there with a suit bag in his hand.

'Georgie asked me to drop this off to you for your dress. The stewards are all busy.'

Libby wanted to slam the door shut, partly from embarrassment and lingering anger but mainly from feelings she wished she didn't have for the man. But she knew that would be bad manners considering he had brought her the suit bag to transport her dress to the party. Words had temporarily escaped her but suddenly she realised that if she reached for the bag, there was a very real possibility she might lose her towel. Libby had no choice but to invite Daniel into her stateroom.

'Um…er…please come in. You can leave the bag over there,' she said, motioning towards the chair beside the desk. 'I'll just finish getting ready so please let yourself out.' With that, Libby crossed the room, her heart racing and her head spinning again, and stepped inside the bathroom. She slipped on the large guest bathrobe behind the door to make her feel less exposed as she stepped back out, determined to send him on his way. She had to be firm and set boundaries—for her own good because she was scared by her reaction to him.

'I appreciate you bringing the suit bag, but I don't want to hold you up,' she told him, trying to hide how self-conscious she felt. 'Georgie told me you're tending to Walter today while I'm helping her so it looks like we'll both be busy.'

'Yes, we will,' he began. 'But it wasn't just the bag that brought me here. We need to talk.'

'I think we did that yesterday and nothing really changed. Lunch was lovely and I enjoyed your company, but you have a complicated life. And that makes two of us,' she said, closing her robe even tighter around her otherwise naked body. She felt vulnerable to her own feelings with Daniel so close. 'Let's leave it at that, Daniel, for the moment. There's something I want to talk to you about but now is not the time.'

'I agree. Yesterday proved to me that we need to talk about what happened so we can have closure.'

'Fine, whatever you think, Daniel. Please just go. We can talk about it another day. I have to help Georgie prepare for the party and I'm running late.'

Libby shut the bathroom door on Daniel as her fingers reached for the locket around her neck. Her heart was racing as she accepted that all hope for them was gone in an instant. He wanted closure. Not that it should have come as a surprise since he had not reached out since leaving but it did sound very final. She held the locket tightly in her clasped hands, praying that she was doing the right thing for Billy's sake by telling Daniel he was a father. Perhaps that closure would include walking away from the son he had never met but if so it would be best to know now.

Disappointed he had not been able to speak with Libby, Daniel headed back to the bridge to check the arrival time with the captain. He needed to have Walter ready for the party and had offered to assist him to dress. Daniel had lain awake until the early hours of the morning, thinking about Libby. She was so close and yet so far from his reach. He wanted to step back in time and do everything differently but that wasn't possible. He had allowed himself to fall for her when he'd had no right to do so. And no right to let Libby believe he was free.

Each moment in such close proximity to her had been torture to him. Knowing she was in the suite next to his, breathing softly as she'd slept, had made his body ache to hold her. He'd ached to tell her how much she meant to him and that his feelings would never change, no matter how far apart they were, but that was unfair. She needed to be free to move on.

He'd tossed and turned in the huge lonely bed as he'd thought back to how natural it would have felt to reach for her hand as they'd strolled around Martinique. How easily he could have kissed her while waiting to order their food and how much he'd wanted to pull her into his arms as they'd walked barefoot across the warm sand. She was everything he wanted and couldn't have.

It had been three a.m., the yacht being tossed about in unruly waves, and Daniel had been no closer to sleep than when he'd climbed into bed four hours before. The Caribbean seas could be temperamental but that had never bothered him before. He had become accustomed to rough water and strong winds. Sleep had never evaded him in bad weather the way it had for the last five days in the calmest of waters. Thoughts of Libby had been keeping him awake. Thoughts of what he had done and how much he continued to hurt her by keeping the truth from her.

Daniel had decided, before finally succumbing to sleep, that he could not live with himself knowing he had caused the sadness and confusion so evident in Libby's beautiful eyes. It would be unfair to let that continue when he had the power to change it. Or at least temper it a little. He would let Libby know enough about his life so that she understood his feelings were real and that the reason he had left was just as real. He would explain his role in Chezlovinka and the need for him to return to take over from his father.

Just spending a few days with Libby had made Daniel realise he could trust her to keep the secret of his father's illness and that it was imperative he return to his homeland—a principality so obscure she would know nothing about it. But at least she would know he did care for her and that what they had shared had been real. It just couldn't be for ever. Her life was in San Francisco, his was a life of serving his people on another continent but the time they had spent together would always be in his heart. She deserved to know that much.

He just had to find the perfect time to tell her before that time ran out.

CHAPTER ELEVEN

LIBBY DRESSED QUICKLY in shorts and a T-shirt and hung her party dress in the suit bag behind the door with her gold sandals, a small gold evening clutch and some long emerald costume jewellery earrings that Bradley had packed. All the while, Libby was thinking about Daniel and wishing that anyone but him had been the ship's doctor.

Her life could have remained simple but at least there were a few days until she told Daniel everything…and he told her whatever it was he had kept from her.

Then they would both, according to him, have closure. Libby wasn't so sure.

As she zipped up the suit bag, she thought that Georgie and Bradley should have their own make-over show called 'How to save the poor nurse with zero styling ability and a million things on her mind'.

Georgie was already under way with the desserts when Libby arrived in the galley.

'How many tarts have you baked?' Libby asked, astonished at the sight of a galley stacked to the ceiling with handmade individual pastry cases.

'Two hundred.'

'For one hundred and fifty guests?'

'You never know, they may like a second and Walter doesn't want anyone missing out on his favourite dessert—Persian custard tartlet with mango, papaya and guava.'

'That sounds exotic and delicious. What can I do to help?'

'It would be wonderful if you could cut up the fruit the way I have done as an example,' Georgie said as she began to make the custard filling with more cream and eggs being taken from the cool room than Libby had seen in her entire local supermarket.

Libby spied the cut fruit resting on a chopping board. It looked perfectly presented. Libby knew her work was cut out for her to ensure her fruit looked as lovely. She reached for an apron and began to peel the first of dozens of mangoes. 'What about the savoury food? Please tell me you're—or *we're*—not preparing that as well?'

'Good God no.' Georgie laughed. 'The

chefs in the resort are preparing that part of the menu.'

'That's a relief,' Libby said as she put the first peeled mango in the huge bowl in front of her and tried to push away thoughts of Daniel and the conversation they would have before the end of the cruise.

The two women and a galley hand spent the next few hours preparing the different elements of the fruit tarts and packing them away in the cool room for transportation to the resort when they docked. Libby had seen the engagement cake resting in the cool room and it was magnificent. Once upon a time she had dreamed of an engagement party and a wedding, both with stunning cakes and all the trimmings, but now she didn't believe in happily ever after.

The chief stewardess arrived to alert them that the yacht would be docking in fifteen minutes. This gave the team time to pack everything ready to be transported to the cool rooms at the resort. It would be like another military operation with everything cut and carefully placed in containers along with three enormous pots of custard that had been chilling.

'When will you do all of the work putting two hundred desserts together?'

'Once we dock, I'll follow the crew to the resort and once mains are served I will begin final preparation. I don't like to chill the pastry so I keep the other ingredients cold and construct and plate the dessert at the last minute. It's so much nicer to bite through room-temperature pastry into a chilled filling. It just adds that bespoke touch at the end of the meal, and Walter loves it done that way.'

'You're such a fussy pants, aren't you?' Libby joked with her friend as they busily gathered everything and stacked it all safely on a trolley for collection by crew members. 'But so is Walter. He loves the whole regalia of uniformed crew and it does look lovely, I must admit.'

'It's the little touches that make the difference,' Georgie replied with an expression that showed she was ready for battle. The engagement cake had to be transported too and Libby could see that was weighing on Georgie's mind. This was a huge event and a lot of the focus would be on the work undertaken by Georgie.

'It will be the best engagement party that San Lucia has ever seen,' Libby said.

'I have a feeling that tonight will absolutely be a night to remember for everyone!' Georgie responded with a wink.

* * *

Daniel assisted Walter to dress for the party. The proud uncle was wearing a tuxedo and bow-tie and requested Daniel do the same.

'The invitation says black tie, so I will truss up like a turkey for the next few hours only because I'll never hear the end of it from Sophia if I don't...and because that is what Contessa would expect of me.'

Daniel noticed Walter turn away abruptly as he spoke and he suspected it was to hide a tear or two.

'It will be a wonderful night, Walter. Everyone will have the best time and you're looking very suave,' Daniel told him. 'Sophia will be proud and Contessa will without doubt be watching all of the celebrations with you.'

'Hmm, do you think so?'

'Absolutely.'

'All right, enough of the mushy stuff,' Walter said gruffly, and he brushed non-existent lint from his jacket sleeves and crossed to the door of the largest suite on the yacht. 'Let's get this show on the road. I think it will be a night to remember.'

The party had begun and Libby stood in the perfect, balmy night air, looking around in amazement at the most beautiful setting she had ever seen. Fairy lights were strung across four giant pontoons only a few metres from shore. Two of the pontoons had tables and chairs, one had a dance floor and there was one for the band, and all four were joined by arched bridges that were also lit by fairy lights and covered in an array of brightly coloured Caribbean flowers, including hundreds of enormous coral-coloured hibiscus flowers. It was a sudden splash of colour and a stark contrast to the predominantly white decor.

The pontoons were secured by large pylons driven through the water and deep into the sand so they didn't shift with the movement of the tide that gently lapped beneath. It was postcard perfect and Libby was standing guard in front of the most stunning engagement cake that she thought had ever been made by anyone anywhere in the world. It was divine in every aspect and Libby was still amazed that it had made it onto the floating pontoon without dislodging one piece of the delicate filigree flowers that cascaded down the five layers like a waterfall of pastel shades of coral tipped with gold leaf over a naked Belgian chocolate torte. It was a piece of art and Libby had watched Walter look over more than once or twice with a smile born of pride in Georgie's work.

Georgie had also been correct in saying that stray hands might be tempted to touch the cake and the potential perpetrators were just as she had expected—the extended family that had sailed in with Walter. Libby had to be firm in reminding them to keep their fingers away from it.

Sophia and her fiancé, Etienne, arrived and the party was soon in full swing. Sophia wore a striking coral-coloured dress that skimmed her shoulders and fell to the floor and her blonde hair was styled in a high ponytail secured with a silk hibiscus flower encrusted with diamonds. Her fiancé was wearing a tuxedo, as were all of the men at the event. Libby thought Walter's niece looked absolutely beautiful and she told him as much when he passed by.

'Thank you. I told you she's the spitting image of her mother.' Then, stepping back and running his gaze over Libby, he added, 'And you look very beautiful yourself.'

'Why, thank you, Walter.'

'But I'm still not completely sold on her fiancé,' Walter leaned in and whispered in her ear. 'He's an actor apparently but I've been told I don't get a choice in the matter.'

'He seems lovely and the way he looks at her shows he is a man in love, and that thought should bring you comfort.'

Walter nodded. 'I guess when you pare everything back, finding true love is all that really matters in life.'

'Yes, it is.'

Walter reached for Libby's hands in a fatherly way. 'Tell me, my dear, are you married? I know you have a little boy but you never mentioned a husband neither do you wear a ring.'

'No, I'm single.'

'Not met the right man yet?' he asked with an impish wink as he sipped on his lime and soda.

'I thought I'd met him but he had other ideas. It's complicated.'

'All matters of the heart are complicated but, just between you and me, if you're looking for a potential boyfriend, I think Dr Daniel is more than a bit keen on you. I've seen the way he looks at you when no one's watching. It's all happened quite quickly since you only met on my yacht, but that level of emotion can't be feigned. It was love at first sight for Contessa and myself so I never judge the speed at which Cupid's arrow hits,' he said with a wink.

'Anyway, I'm not sure how you feel about him, but his face lights up when anyone mentions your name. I've not raised it with him because it's not my place, and he's a bit of a closed book. I thought I'd test my theory yesterday so I asked him to accompany you to Martinique and, just as I thought, he jumped at the chance. I'm quite intuitive when it comes to people. You know, Libby, he's not a bad looking rooster and you'd have medicine as a common interest. You could do worse… if you're in the market for a husband, I mean.'

'I'm not in the market,' she snapped quickly.

'Well, maybe not now, but keep our Dr Daniel in mind for the future. Who knows, he might grow on you. It took me a while to win my gorgeous wife but eventually she fell in love with me. Anyway, enough of my matchmaking, I'd best be off and mingle with all the other guests… And by the way, you're doing a wonderful job keeping Contessa's relatives away from the cake. Georgie told me you were on duty. Excellent job, keep it up.'

Libby felt her back stiffen, her heart begin to race and her thoughts become airborne swirling above her, unable to be reined in. She was having a fight-or-flight response to what Walter had told her before he'd rushed off to mingle with the guests. It was fortunate he had left her alone because she was both stunned and speechless.

Just when Libby thought their conversation about Daniel was finished, Walter came back. 'By the way, he's looking your way from over at the bar. You've certainly got him mesmerised…and a man mesmerised is a man in love.'

Libby instantly turned to see Daniel standing at the bar with a drink in his hand. His smile widened and as much as she didn't want to smile back, her lips seemed to take on a mind of their own and curled upwards. He looked so handsome in his tuxedo. But Libby had to admit that Daniel looked handsome in anything he wore…and even more handsome when he wore nothing.

Suddenly, she was so angry at herself for having romantic thoughts about Daniel. In fact, any thoughts about him. He was a closed book—even Walter agreed about that part and the rest of what he'd said was disturbing. She turned her attention back to the cake and away from him. Guarding the cake was her job for the night until Sophia and her fiancé cut it, and then she could return to the yacht and close the door on the world.

It wasn't long before the happy couple made their way to the cake. Mains had finished and the Persian tartlets arrived and were quickly devoured by all the guests, with a number asking for seconds, including Walter. Libby took a few small steps backwards as the couple posed for the photographs by the professional photographer and guests alike. She hadn't realised how close she was to the edge of the pontoon but that soon became evident. Her stomach sank with the realisation that her left heel was off the pontoon and hovering over the water. Suddenly, she lost her balance and with her arms flapping ungraciously she fell backwards into the water. There were gasps from the guests and Walter signalled the band to stop playing. Daniel sprinted from the bar where he had been standing most of the night and dived into the water in his tuxedo. While it wasn't overly deep or cold, it was eerily dark and the moment Libby felt Daniel's strong arms around her, she felt safe. Humiliated but safe.

'Are you all right?' he asked as he gently swept away the damp curls clinging to her face.

'I'm fine thank you...' she began, trying to catch her breath. 'But I can't believe you did that. Your tuxedo is drenched now and we both look silly. You should've let me look silly on my own.'

Daniel smiled. 'You don't look silly, you look beautiful. I've wanted to tell you just how beautiful you looked all night. Now you look wet and beautiful.'

Libby looked back at him in silence and realised just why she had fallen in love with him. And why it had been impossible to forget him.

'Is everything okay?' Walter called out from the edge of the pontoon, where he stood surrounded by an army of concerned guests, including Sophia and Etienne.

'We're fine, just felt like a late-night swim,' Daniel said as he took Libby's hand and led her from the water to shore. 'We might head back to the yacht...for some dry clothes.'

Libby didn't remember much about the walk back to the marina and the yacht. With Daniel's hand still holding hers, she felt like she was home even though she was four thousand miles from San Francisco. She couldn't pull her hand free despite how much she knew she should. She was tired of doing everything alone and she loved feeling protected. Perhaps she was making another mistake, she wasn't sure, but at that moment it felt right. Her heart felt light and she couldn't remember ever feeling this happy.

* * *

Finally, they reached the *Coral Contessa* and one of the stewards, who must have seen them making their way towards the yacht, greeted them with two large white towels.

'Late-night dip?'

'Something like that,' Daniel said as he wrapped one of the towels around Libby and pulled her close.

The steward departed as quietly as he had arrived, leaving them alone on the deck. Daniel looked at Libby and knew it was time to tell her everything. He cared deeply for her and he knew in his heart he could trust her. She had given him no reason not to trust her. He wanted her to know everything. He knew it wouldn't change the outcome but she deserved to know it all.

His family was going to have him for the rest of his life so he deserved to give Libby what she needed to move on with hers. Daniel looked into the blackness of the star-filled sky. The dark canvas above them was dotted with tiny sparkling beacons of hope and, while there were none in Daniel's mind, he knew he was doing the right thing.

'You have to stop saving me,' Libby said softly. 'You're starting to make a habit of it.

First rescuing me from Maxwell and now Caribbean sharks.'

Daniel smiled. He would willingly rescue Libby for the rest of his life if he could. But he couldn't.

'I want to tell you something, Libby.' He turned to her and began, 'It's something I've wanted to tell you for a very long time and I tried to tell you this morning.'

'That you actually still care for me and that's why you jumped into the water to save me?'

'That…and something else…'

'If it's true that you still care for me then the something else can wait until tomorrow,' she told him as she stood up and looked into his eyes. 'Let's not talk any more…let's just have tonight and talk about the rest tomorrow.'

Daniel was surprised but he didn't want to argue. He felt the same way. He hadn't made any promises and he never would. Libby knew that, and yet she wanted to spend the night with him and he wanted her more than words could say. What he needed to tell her could wait until the morning.

His arms reached for her like a man possessed, his mouth hovering inches from hers.

'Are you sure?' he asked, his voice low and husky.

Libby nodded and with her head tilted upwards she stood on tiptoe to meet his lips. Unable to wait a moment longer, his mouth met hers with a tenderness and urgency that she returned. His hands gently roamed the curves of her still-damp body as their kisses become more passionate. Her back arched against the hardness of his body and his lips began to trail kisses down her neck. Within moments, Daniel scooped her into his arms and she buried her head against his chest as he carried her to his suite and to the bed that would be theirs for the night.

CHAPTER TWELVE

DANIEL WOKE IN the morning with Libby lying naked in his arms and he wished with all of his heart he could wake that way for ever. Gently she stirred and, turning to face him, she smiled the most angelic smile he had ever seen.

'Good morning,' he whispered, and kissed her tenderly.

'Good morning, yourself,' she said, and kissed him back.

Daniel rolled onto his back and looked towards the ceiling while Libby rested her head on his chest. 'Would you like some breakfast?'

'No,' she murmured. 'I'm fine right here. I don't want to leave bed, it means we have to face reality and I'm not ready yet.'

Daniel turned his face away and looked into the distance. He had to agree, but he also had to tell Libby the truth.

'Nor me,' he told her with a melancholy tone to his voice. 'It couldn't be more perfect but there's something I do need to tell you. I tried to last night…'

'I know,' she said. 'I'm sorry I stopped you.'

'I'm very glad you did,' he said, kissing her softly. 'But now we really do need to talk. It's important that you know everything.'

'I have something I need to tell you too, Daniel,' Libby began.

Daniel smiled a bitter-sweet smile, knowing he would love to spend his life learning everything there was about Libby, but instead he had to tell her the harsh realities of his so they truly could have closure.

'To understand why I did what I did four years ago, you need to know about my background, where I came from—'

'I'm not going to judge you by where you grew up,' Libby interrupted him, and stroked his arm. 'I don't believe in that whole "born on the wrong side of the tracks" idea. I think you are what you make of yourself; it's not where you came from.'

Daniel couldn't help but smile again at what Libby had said. She obviously thought he came from a disadvantaged background and was trying to make him feel better. Her heart was huge and accepting and she didn't have a judgmental bone in her gorgeous body. He couldn't have loved her more and that made it all so very sad. Libby deserved better than a life with him.

'No, Libby, I didn't struggle growing up. In fact, it was quite the opposite. I grew up with great privilege.'

'I see,' she said with a curious look on her face. 'What sort of privilege? An elite school and a nanny?'

'Yes…and some.'

'And some?'

'My family is the royal family of a small principality in Europe.'

'You're a member of a royal family?' she asked in an incredulous tone. 'An actual royal family?'

'Yes, but it's not a huge country. I doubt you've heard of it. My Father is the Crown Prince of Chezlovinka.'

'Chezlovinka? The principality that borders Greece.'

'You've heard of it?'

'Yes, I've heard of it,' she replied with curiosity on her face as she propped herself up on the pillow and looked into his eyes. 'I studied it in my final year of college.'

'You studied Chezlovinka?'

'Yes, it's a beautiful Mediterranean country…' Libby paused, her eyes wide with shock and a little disbelief. 'But I never saw any images of you.'

'My mother was very protective and she kept me from the scrutiny of the media so I could have a relatively normal childhood and early adult life. She was the one who encouraged me to pursue medicine. I studied in London.'

Libby was silent for a moment. 'Oh, my God, that means you're a prince.'

'Yes,' he nodded. 'Prince Daniel Dimosa.'

'So that's what this is all about. Now it makes sense,' she said, pulling the covers up around her and moving away. Her forehead wrinkled with a frown as she stared at Daniel. 'You're a prince and I'm a commoner. I get it. You need a princess and I'm a long way from that.'

'No, Libby, you're not a long way from that. You're kind and intelligent and empathetic and everything a princess needs to be, but there's a dark side to the story, as there always is in fairy tales. My life isn't about palaces and joy. It will be filled with sacrifice and duty and I don't want you to have to sacrifice anything in life. I want you to have everything you want and I can't give you that.'

'I understand, Daniel. You're letting me down gently,' she said softly as she closed her eyes.

'No,' Daniel said, reaching for her and pulling her close again. 'That's not it at all, Libby. You're far too good for the life I could give you.'

'That's sweet, Daniel, but it's not true. You will have a wonderful life there.'

'It is true, Libby.'

'You don't have to say anything else, Daniel. I wouldn't fit in to your royal lifestyle and you can't fit back into mine. My life is simple. I'm just a nurse from San Francisco.'

'Don't say that,' he cut in firmly. 'You're the most amazing woman I've ever met and I would fly to the end of the earth for you, but a life with me is not one I would wish on anyone. Least of all you.'

'You're a wonderful man, Daniel. I understand that you wanted to protect me from the scrutiny of a life that you are very accustomed to but one that's a very long way from mine,' she said as she moved away a little and looked at the ceiling fan gently circling above them. 'You need a woman who comes from the same place in society, not a woman who may be a liability. You don't need a woman clumsy enough to fall off a pontoon and embarrass you.'

'Libby, you could never embarrass me. And I would dive off a million pontoons for you but it's not about you. It's about my family.'

Libby reached for the towel on the floor and slipped from the bed and into the bathroom and returned in a bathrobe.

'Your family? What do you mean?' she asked as she began to collect her clothes from the floor.

'It's my father. He's not well and I need to return to take over the country. I knew it would happen one day and that's why I didn't want to become involved with you. I'm sorry I lost the ability to see reason and walk away. I was selfish to want one night with you. It was unfair and I had no right, but a part of me was in denial.'

'I guess I understand. It's sort of how I behaved last night… I just wanted one night with you and to hell with the consequences.'

'And, believe me, I'm glad you did, but one night is all it can be. I'm sorry.'

'I know it was just one night. You said upfront you wanted closure between us and I'm a big girl. I went into last night knowing that. You have nothing to be sorry about.' Her voice was still barely more than a whisper and filled with sadness.

'I told you yesterday when we were on Martinique that my life was not my own to live. It's not mine to make my own choices—many have been made for me by virtue of being a member of the royal family and some by virtue of being my father's son.'

'Isn't that one and the same?'

'Not quite, but I must return home. My father's condition will never improve. There's no medication or treatment that can change the prognosis.'

'Is your father's illness terminal?' she asked as she sat on the edge of the bed just out of his reach.

'Yes, but we have no idea how long he has left. My father's is a cruel fate because he has early onset familial Alzheimer's disease. He's wasting away inside his own body.'

Daniel suddenly felt relieved saying it aloud to Libby. He hadn't told anyone before and now he had it was as if half the weight of the world had been lifted from his shoulders. Nothing had changed, and nor would it, but he felt more at peace than ever before. He had never expected to feel that way. He'd thought he would feel tortured and racked with guilt for betraying the family, but it was as if he had been betraying Libby for the longest time by not letting her know.

Libby's expression fell into one of all-consuming sadness. 'Oh, Daniel, that is so very sad. I'm so sorry. I can only imagine how hard it must be on you and your mother and everyone around them.'

'It's been difficult but my father has been able to manage until now. It's been an early onset but also a slow onset. But the symptoms have worsened over the last month so my mother sent for me. I will be heading there next week. I can't delay my return any longer.'

'The people of Chezlovinka must also be saddened by the news of your father's illness.'

'That's just it,' Daniel said with a resoluteness to his voice. 'They can't know. I have to step up and take control so my father can quietly abdicate and keep his dignity. It would cause doubt in their minds about him and about me and about the future of the country. There's been too much unrest in the world lately to bring more uncertainty to them now.'

'I understand you don't want to upset them with news of your father but why do you say the same about yourself? It's a disease afflicting your father, not you.'

'That's just it, Libby. It could affect me. My

father's condition is caused by a mutation in a single gene and a single copy of the mutant gene inherited from either parent will cause the disease in the child. There is every chance I have inherited the mutated gene and my life in a few years may be just like his.'

'But you don't know that for sure.'

'No, but I also have no guarantee it won't and the people of Chezlovinka are not naive. If they learn the nature of my father's illness, they will quickly work out that it's genetic and one day in the future I too may be affected. They need stability and that's why I will head back to my country and begin grooming my successor so that in the event I do succumb to the disease, he can ascend to the throne.

'I have looked into altering the constitution to allow my adopted paternal cousin, Edward, who is studying law at Cambridge, to reign over the principality. Because he was adopted at birth by my father's brother and his wife, there would be no risk of the disease continuing in the family but he would carry on the Dimosa name.'

'And you have to keep this secret to yourself.'

'Not entirely. I can't. My father has deteriorated to a point now that he has a loyal team of nurses who have all agreed to assist and say nothing outside the palace walls.'

'But what about you? You must know how I feel about you. I can be there for you, if you'll let me.'

'You're the most wonderful woman, Libby, and you know how I feel about you too, but I can't ask you to do that. I can't ask you to give up the life you have and risk spending your life caring for me. I don't want that life for you. I don't want you to have to look after me the way my mother has looked after my father and will continue to nurse a man who soon may not even recognise her.'

'But you may not have the condition, Daniel. And if you did it wouldn't change the way I feel about you.'

'It would change everything to me,' he said. 'I can't allow you to risk being trapped with a man who is trapped inside himself.'

Daniel wanted to add *And one who didn't want children*. Libby would be the most wonderful mother and he wasn't prepared to risk having a child who might also carry the gene. Daniel was adamant he wouldn't be tested until he showed symptoms. No good would come of learning his fate early. He felt certain that he would not have been spared the same destiny as his father and he didn't want his mother to have the worry of her only child being trapped like her husband. If he didn't have the test, he didn't have to lie to his mother about the prognosis.

Libby wiped the tears that were spilling down her cheeks. 'If you truly care for me, why don't you let me make that decision?'

'I'm giving you the chance to find a man who comes without the risk of a disease that will rob you of a long and happy life. I don't want you to be a care-giver. You should be a man's wife and lover for ever without the risks that being with me would carry.'

'It wouldn't change my feelings for you whatever the result but if it's forcing you to make this decision to shut me out, why won't you get tested? You would know what the future held and then be able to make rational decisions based on fact.'

Daniel drew a deep breath. 'I will be tested one day but not now. I need to be strong for my family and my country. I need to focus on them and not me. If it was confirmed now that I had the gene for early onset familial Alzheimer's disease, then every day I would live with that knowledge and I would not be able to hide that from my mother. It would not be fair to add further to her worries. She shouldn't lie awake concerned about both of the men in her life.'

'I do understand, but perhaps not knowing is also a worry for your mother...'

'Maybe I'm being selfish, Libby, but if I learn the truth, and it's as I suspect it will be, then I may not have a single moment of peace. I will live my life in fear of how it will play out.'

'But, Daniel,' she told him, 'that's how you're living your life now.'

Daniel looked at Libby in silence, considering her words...and wondering if she was right.

Libby reached for her locket as Daniel climbed from the warmth of the bed in silence and, slipping on a bathrobe, stood by the window, looking out to sea.

'There's something I need to share with you,' she said as she followed suit and climbed from the bed. Pulling the sheet around her, she crossed to him. 'Something that may change the way you feel about everything. About your future...and even about being tested.'

Daniel turned back to her and held her tightly to him. 'There's nothing in the world that can change my future, no matter how much I wish it to be true. And I will not consider testing until it's absolutely necessary. I need to think of my mother and my country, not myself, at this time. I'm sorry, Libby, but there's nothing you could say that would change how I feel or what lies ahead for me.'

'I disagree. I know there is.' She began stepping back and started to open the locket that hung around her neck, the one that held the picture of Daniel's son, *their* son, who looked so very much like his father.

Suddenly the yacht was tossed by a wave with such force it sent Libby back into his arms. 'Are you all right?'

'I… I think so,' she stammered. 'I've never felt anything like that. Are we going to be all right? That was a huge wave. The water hit the window and we're on the top deck.'

'We're back out in the Atlantic Ocean, and I'm guessing there must be bad weather ahead. Please sit down. Don't leave the cabin,' he began as he grabbed some casual trousers and a shirt from the closet and dressed quickly, looking outside to see ominous dark clouds had overtaken the sky. 'I'll head to the bridge and check with the captain to see what's happening. I'll also call in to see Walter on the way. I shouldn't be long.'

'Please don't forget I need to speak with

you,' Libby said as she sat down, still draped in a sheet. 'It's important.'

'We'll talk, I promise, as soon as I get back.'

CHAPTER THIRTEEN

Daniel checked his watch as he closed the door to his cabin where he had left Libby. It was seven o'clock and the scheduled time to give Walter his daily early morning medical check. He made his way to the master suite at the end of the corridor, all the while being tossed from side to side with the motion of the yacht in the waves. His arms were outstretched and he kept his balance with his hands firmly against the corridor walls.

Suddenly, he realised it had been the first day he hadn't checked the time upon waking. It was his habit to check and plan the day but that morning, with Libby so close, knowing the time had been the last thing on his mind. But everything he had told her weighed heavily on him—not that she would betray his trust but that she wouldn't accept his resolute position on setting her free.

He had a swipe card to open the door in

an emergency and when there was no answer to his knocking, he did just that, but quietly. Walter, he found, was still sleeping and it appeared that the waves tossing the *Coral Contessa* about hadn't broken his slumber. Daniel let him be. He had heard the guests rowdily return in the early hours and had assumed Walter would have been one of them, so he was not surprised that his patient was still happily asleep under his covers.

Daniel guessed that most of the other guests would be doing the same, as they had both eaten and drunk themselves merry in San Lucia.

The captain had made mention the night before that they would be heading off at six in the morning for two days at sea on their way back to Miami, so they would be able to sleep off the effects of the party for forty-eight hours if necessary, but Daniel was concerned that with the rough weather he might need to check on the nausea medication supplies after he visited the bridge. Then he would return to Libby so they could continue their talk. While it wouldn't change anything, he wanted to spend every last minute of this time with her before they parted for ever. It felt good that there were no secrets any more. It was how it should be.

* * *

Daniel arrived at the bridge and received an update on the weather from the captain. They were in the tail end of a storm that was heading south and further out to sea, but they were still feeling the effects of the waves.

'We're on the clean side of the storm,' Eric told him, dividing his concentration between the navigation panel and the undulating horizon ahead. 'Unless there's a sudden change, we'll have the shallower waves and lower winds this side. We're surrounded by thirteen thousand tons of yacht so there's not much risk to us.'

'So we shouldn't be concerned about the waves hitting the top deck a little while ago,' Daniel said, remembering the force that had thrown Libby off balance.

'Before the storm shifted southerly, we were slammed by towering walls of water but they've subsided now and the skies should clear up soon. The seas will still be a little rough for another two hours but nothing as severe as we've just encountered. After that, it should be smooth sailing back to Miami. However, I've asked the stewards to inform guests not to go out onto their balconies for the next few hours until I give the all clear.'

'Do you think they would actually consider doing that in this weather?'

'You'd be surprised,' Eric said, rolling his eyes but still looking ahead.

A steward appeared at that moment to inform Daniel that a guest had been thrown from his bed in the last big wave, lacerating his head. He was bleeding profusely and another thought she had a sprained ankle after falling on the way to the bathroom. Concerned there might be more injuries over the next two hours in the rough seas, exacerbated by the effects of the too much alcohol at the party, Daniel needed Libby to assist him. He knew she had her pager, so he sent her a message and asked her if she could change and head to the infirmary as soon as she could while he left the bridge and headed to get his medical bag and then go to the head injury patient first.

Within minutes, Daniel was at the first patient call and knocked on the cabin door. A clearly distraught woman opened it and invited Daniel inside. 'There's so much blood. I think he'll need stitches,' she told him as she took a sip from her wine glass.

Daniel could see the injured man sitting on the bed slightly slouched over. He appeared to be in his late sixties and was holding a white hand towel on the area over his left eye. There didn't appear to be too much blood on the makeshift bandage.

Daniel opened his medical bag, donned gloves and with some sterile swabs crossed to the man.

'I'm Daniel and I'm the ship's doctor. You've no doubt seen me around the ship. What's your name?'

The man looked him up and down. 'I'm Stan and I've not seen you on the yacht but I saw you dive into the water last night. That was an odd thing to do at a party.'

'It was very peculiar, I agree,' the woman chimed in.

Daniel chose to ignore their comments. 'Let's look at your injury, Stan. If you could drop your hand, I'd like to take a look at the cut.'

Slowly the man released the pressure he was applying to the towel and Daniel leaned in, prepared to see a deep wound, but instead found there was a slight abrasion. A graze of sorts. There was little sign of bleeding.

Daniel wiped the area with the swab. 'Would you like me to cover the skin with a dressing?'

'You're not stitching the wound?' the woman asked with the glass still in her hand.

'I think he needs stitches or he might start bleeding again. He could bleed all over the cabin.'

'Yeah, you should just stitch it and be done with it,' Stan agreed.

'There's nothing that requires stitches...'

'Are you sure?' the woman asked as she swayed with the movement of the yacht, though that wasn't the only reason for her inability to stand upright and perhaps for Stan falling out of bed. Daniel could see a small pile of minibar-size bottles of liquor on the dresser. It appeared that the party had continued in their room. He applied an adhesive dressing to the clean area and reassured them that the injury was not as serious as they had first thought. He left their cabin and called instructions through to the stewards to keep an eye on the pair and perhaps not refill the minibar that day.

Daniel arrived at the infirmary to find Libby inside with another guest.

'When did the nausea begin?' he heard Libby ask the man as she drew closer.

'When the big wave hit, we both started throwing up.'

Daniel looked around but there was no one else there. 'You said *we*. Is there someone else suffering from nausea?'

'Yes, my wife, but she didn't want to come down. She decided to go out on the balcony and get some fresh air. She thought it might help.'

'In this weather? She's out on her balcony? Which room?'

'The first deck, cabin nine.'

Daniel raced to the phone and called for a steward to head to the room immediately and he did the same, leaving Libby to attend to the man's nausea. Daniel needed to check on the man's wife. There was still another two hours of bad weather and rough seas ahead and Daniel didn't want anyone on their balcony, particularly if they'd spent the night drinking. The steward was already at cabin door nine, already knocking when Daniel arrived.

There was no answer so Daniel used his swipe card to open the door and, just as he had feared, the woman was leaning over the railing and vomiting. He crossed the room with long purposeful steps and pulled her inside just as a large wave slammed the yacht. It was low on the side but still powerful and Daniel and the steward shook their heads in unison, both aware that it could have ended very differently if they hadn't arrived in time.

'Can you knock on every cabin door and

remind guests again that they are not to step outside under any circumstances? And don't refill any minibars until we dock in Miami.'

Daniel then headed to see his next patient with the suspected sprained ankle. He arrived to find Stella lying on the bed with her foot elevated. He looked around the room and was relieved to see no sign of empty bottles. Stella was in her early forties and travelling with her mother, who had headed off to bring her back some breakfast. Daniel remembered seeing them both dancing at the party. On close examination of her ankle, foot and lower leg, he could see it had been damaged in the fall. There were a number of points of tenderness and pain when she attempted even the slightest movement.

'It appears to be just a sprain, Stella, so I'd advise you to rest and avoid movement that causes discomfort. I'll order up some more ice and I'd like you to pack that around your ankle for about twenty minutes and repeat that every two or three hours during the day.'

'Better today than yesterday. I would have missed the party and the dancing…and seeing you dive into the water in your tuxedo to save your wife.'

Daniel said nothing. Libby was not his wife

and never would be. Spending the night with her in his arms had made the thought of saying goodbye and never seeing her beautiful face again overwhelming but he had the next two days with her and he intended to make the most of that time.

'Should I see my doctor when I get back to New York?' Stella asked.

'If the pain's not subsiding after a day or so I would definitely make an appointment with your GP. He may need to arrange an X-ray or MRI. However, I'll return later to check on you and I may compress your ankle with an elastic bandage to manage any swelling and we will have a better idea if you have sustained a fracture, but at this time I believe it's just sprained.'

After ordering an ice pack for Stella, Daniel headed back to check on Walter. He was his most important patient and had been left alone in the rough weather. He apologised when he arrived at Walter's suite.

'I'm fine,' Walter told him. 'I'm an old sea dog. I quite like it when the sea gets angry and tosses us about. It's invigorating. Lets you know you're alive.'

Daniel wasn't convinced but didn't argue the point. He just checked Walter's blood pressure and was happy it was still within normal range and the wound was continuing to heal. Perhaps the trip to the Caribbean was just what the doctor should have ordered.

'So how did the pair of you dry out after your midnight swim?' Walter asked as Daniel closed his medical bag and slipped off the latex gloves. 'Quite heroic of you to dive in like that.'

'It was only a few feet of water...'

'That's not the point. Women love to be saved and I'm sure Libby appreciated your chivalry,' he said, smiling. 'I did notice you two didn't come back to the party. I assume you took the time to become better acquainted.'

'We decided to stay on the yacht and talk,' Daniel said, running his lean fingers along his chin.

'I hope you stepped up and finally kissed her,' Walter said with one eyebrow slightly raised.

'I'm not telling you—'

'You don't come across a young lady as lovely as Libby more than once in your life,' Walter cut in. 'And I'll take your lack of a denial as a yes. It's about time because I could see you had feelings for her from the moment you met and she'd be perfect for you. I suspected it was a case of love at first sight...'

'Actually, Walter, we knew each other before this cruise.'

'You knew each other? Libby never said a thing to me and I thought I knew everything about her.'

'You know everything about her? You must have spoken to her for longer than I did.'

'Well, I know she lives close to her parents.'

'In San Francisco. It's where we met.'

'She's never travelled much before this trip.'

'I think she's a bit of a homebody,' Daniel said with a smile as he crossed to the door to return to the woman about whom they were speaking.

'And she's the single mother of a three-year-old little boy.'

Daniel stopped in mid-step and his expression was suddenly no longer light-hearted as he turned back to face Walter. 'Libby has a son?'

'Yes. Billy's his name and his birthday's only a few days after mine.'

'Which is when, exactly?'

'January tenth. He had his birthday a few days before we sailed. I told Libby he was an Easter bunny conception like me.'

Daniel felt the blood drain from his face. An Easter conception?

'How old did you say her son was?' Daniel asked.

'Three, she told me.'

Surely not. It couldn't be. His mind was racing. They had slept together on the night of the Easter gala almost four years ago.

'But don't worry, there's no husband. Libby told me she's single. When I asked about the father of her child, she told me it didn't work out. She mentioned something about it being *complicated*.'

Complicated? Daniel rushed from the room without saying another word. He had to find Libby. He had to know if she had been keeping something from him. He'd told her everything about his life and she hadn't told him about her son. Why would she hide that unless it was deliberate? Unless there was a chance the little boy was his son.

Daniel knew she would not be in his suite so he headed to hers. He needed to know why she had been hiding her son from him. He suspected he knew the answer already. He knocked on her door like a man needing the oxygen inside the room to breathe.

After a few moments Libby opened the door and he stepped inside and slammed it closed behind him.

'I know you have a son. I need to know, is he my child?'

Libby was stunned by Daniel's question and the look of fury in his eyes. She had wanted to tell Daniel herself and not have him learn about their son from someone else.

Her heart began to pound inside her chest. Her chin was quivering, tears building by the moment as she nodded her reply.

'Walter told you, didn't he?'

'How I know doesn't matter. I just want to know, is he mine?'

'Yes, Daniel, he's yours. You have a son.'

Suddenly, her reasons for keeping her secret from him for all these days escaped her. She was searching for something that made sense. Something she could tell Daniel that would justify her actions. It all seemed wrong now. Very wrong. She'd had every opportunity to tell him for the last week and she had chosen silence. She told herself that she had been looking for the right time but was there ever going to be a right time? Or had she been looking for a reason not to tell him?

'Was it as simple as just wanting to punish me?' he asked with both anger and sadness colouring his voice.

'No, it wasn't that. I wasn't punishing you—'

'I disagree, Libby. I think you very much

wanted to punish me for leaving you the way I did after we slept together.'

'I was eight weeks pregnant when I found out.'

'Why didn't you contact me then?'

Libby looked at him with her guilt quickly morphing into something closer to resentment. 'By that time you had long gone. As we both know, you'd slipped away before the sun came up the morning after we made love.'

'You could have found me if you wanted to,' he told her without taking his gaze from her.

'How dare you! I tried to find your contact details through the hospital HR records but they were closed. And it was well above my pay grade to request that they be opened. I guess a *prince* can have anything he wants but a commoner like me has to play by the rules.'

Libby was furious at the accusations Daniel was throwing at her. He had no right to put all of the responsibility back on her when he was the one who'd left without saying a word. Or leaving a forwarding address.

'After I left without an explanation, you had every right to be angry,' he replied, softening his tone slightly but still sounding cold and distant. Then just as quickly it grew in harshness as he spoke. 'But keeping me from knowing about a child, Libby, for all these years, that's more than just punishing me. You've been punishing *our* son too.'

Libby felt an ache in her heart as those words slipped from his lips. It was true what had happened, although it had not been deliberate. But the way he had called Billy *our son* brought a sting of tears to her eyes. Now that she knew why he had left, she knew Daniel was not the cold, callous man she had created in her own mind over the years but she couldn't change the past. Nor could he. They had both kept secrets that could tear them apart for ever.

She knew she should have told him after they'd left the engagement party. She should have told him before they'd made love. Or that morning. There were so many times when she should have told him.

'Billy did not deserve to be denied knowing I was his father or I denied knowing I had a son,' he said, pacing the room with long purposeful steps that led nowhere.

'I tried to tell you this morning...'

'So you were only going to tell me because we spent the night together? If that hadn't happened were you going to leave the yacht and not look back? Why didn't you tell me the first day you saw me? Or on Martinique, or any of the other times we were alone? Did you want to cement us, rekindle what we had before telling me?'

'No. I didn't want to rekindle anything with you.'

'I think you did. That's what all of this was about. You wanted to know if we would re-unite before you told me about my son. I re-member you saying, "Let's have the night and to hell with tomorrow." And clearly to hell with me knowing I had a son if it didn't work out between us.'

Libby was furious again with the way he was speaking to her, accusing her of only telling him when she'd got what she wanted. It wasn't true.

'I never said to hell with tomorrow…'

'Maybe not the words but it was what you meant when you said, "Let's have the night."'

'How can you twist my words like that?' she asked, holding back the tears that were building as the accusations poured from his mouth.

'I'm not twisting anything, Libby. I'm tell-ing you how I see it.'

'I wasn't sure you would even care…'

'You had no right to make such a sweeping assumption about me, Libby. You don't know me.'

'That's right, Daniel. I don't really know you because you kept your real life a secret from me. And perhaps there's more you've kept from me.'

Daniel stopped in his tracks and stared across the room at Libby. 'I laid my life bare for you this morning, Libby. Everything was out for you to know. Nothing was hidden because I trusted you and in return you couldn't even tell me that I have a three-year-old son. Now I know my trust was misguided.'

'I was trying to tell you about Billy this morning…'

Daniel shook his head. 'I guess you didn't try hard enough, did you?'

CHAPTER FOURTEEN

DANIEL STAYED IN his cabin with his thoughts for as long as possible. The rough seas had abated and the captain had given the all clear for the passengers to venture onto their balconies again. Daniel spoke to him about the minibars being left unstocked, at least overnight, and they agreed it would be in the best interests of the few somewhat intoxicated passengers in order to ensure they were safe and not likely to do anything silly. They could have a drink with dinner in the dining area but not in their cabins.

Daniel's mind kept wandering back to Libby and her son. Their son. He wanted to know more about the little boy. What he liked to do. What he looked like. His favourite colour and favourite food. Daniel wanted to know everything. But most of all he wanted to know he was safe. Safe from the genetic disease that ran through the Dimosa family.

But that was Daniel's responsibility. Not Libby's or anyone else's.

That lay squarely with him. He knew what he had to do.

Daniel ate his lunch and dinner in his cabin. He didn't want to see anyone. He had so much to think about now. More than he could have ever imagined when he'd set sail on the *Coral Contessa*.

Libby remained in her cabin too. Georgie had called by but Libby had told her friend she was tired and would rather stay inside and they would catch up the next day.

Libby couldn't stop thinking about the angst written all over Daniel's face when he had confronted her. She knew that while she'd had her reasons for keeping Billy a secret initially, she should have told Daniel before he'd discovered it from someone else. She had been the judge and jury and found him guilty three years before and she hadn't lifted that life sentence.

She lay on her bed thinking and rethinking everything from the day they had met until that morning. The tears flowed for what might have been but what was most apparent to Libby was Daniel not asking for proof of his son's paternity. He trusted Libby's word that he was the father. While he was angry and hurt, he had never doubted her the way she had doubted him.

She knew in her heart that Daniel had done the wrong thing for the right reason. He had wanted to protect her from a life in a country far from home, potentially nursing him, and she had repaid that chivalrous behaviour by denying him knowledge of his son, even when she'd had the chance.

Libby didn't expect that Daniel would want to see her again and she wasn't sure how they could move forward but she knew somehow that they would work out visitation for Daniel with Billy. Of that she was certain. Libby knew her first instincts about Daniel had been right all those years ago. He was a good man and she would make sure his son got to know that too.

But there was something else she wanted to do. Daniel deserved to share in Billy's life up to that day. She opened her computer and began the task of piecing together her son's life from the first ultrasound to his third birthday. Every precious moment—Billy's first steps, his first words and everything else that she thought would bring Daniel closer to knowing his son.

It took all night but finally, at seven the next morning, it was complete and saved to a USB that she slipped into an envelope with her number in San Francisco if Daniel wanted to make a time to meet his son. She quietly left it by his door.

It was night time before they docked in Miami and there was a knock on Libby's cabin door. She was almost packed, just leaving out shorts and a top to wear the next day.

She was expecting Georgie as they had arranged for drinks on the deck. While it wasn't something she was keen to do, Libby knew she owed it to her friend.

'One minute,' she called out.

'I will wait as long as it takes,' the deep voice replied.

Libby froze. It was Daniel's voice, not Georgie's. Taking a deep breath to steady her nerves, she tentatively crossed to the door. It took a moment longer for her to open it.

'I didn't expect to see you,' she said honestly.

'I guessed as much as you left your telephone number in the envelope,' he told her without taking his eyes away from hers.

'I thought if you were ever in the area you

might like to call and make a time to meet Billy.'

'I want much more than that,' he said. 'We need to talk. May I come inside?'

Libby nodded and stepped back from the door. Her worst nightmare was about to be realised. Daniel, she surmised, wanted to talk to her about more than visiting his son. There was the very real risk that he might want joint custody. And she knew he had the right to ask for that.

'Every child has the right to know they are loved unconditionally by their parents, no matter how their parents feel about each other,' he began, confirming her suspicions as he crossed to the balcony doors. They were open and the cool evening breeze was softly moving the sheer curtains. Slowly, he turned to face Libby. 'I want our son to know that I will love him until I take my last breath.'

'I know you will, and I'm so sorry, Daniel,' Libby began. 'I know I should have told you but I stupidly thought I was protecting Billy from being hurt. He's my world. He's my everything.'

'Protect him from me? How could you think I would hurt him?'

Libby collapsed back onto the bed, her tears beginning to flow. 'Because you hurt me and I didn't want him to love you the way I did and have you walk away. I couldn't let him know you and love you, only to have you disappear. I thought it would be better for Billy to never have you than to lose you because that is an unbearable pain.'

Daniel looked at Libby in silence and she felt her heart breaking all over again.

'I'm sorry, Daniel, I'm so sorry.'

'You said you loved me. Do you still feel that way? Do you still love me, Libby?' he asked, staring deeply into her eyes as if he was searching her very soul for the answer.

She nodded as she wiped the tears away with her hands.

Without saying another word or asking another question, Daniel crossed to her and gently pulled her up and into his arms.

'Then I should be the one apologising, Libby. I'm sorry I left you that night. I'm sorry I stayed away and I'm sorry I let you down.'

'I know now you had your reasons—'

'None that were good enough to put you through what I did. I've made some calls and I'm taking the genetic test. Not for myself, I'm taking it for Billy and for you. And I swear, if you give me a second chance, I will never disappear again.'

Libby raised her face to him. 'You want a second chance with me?'

'More than anything I have ever wanted.' Daniel's lips hovered very close to hers as he whispered, 'I love you, Libby. I have since the day I met you and I will never stop loving you, if you let me.'

EPILOGUE

LIBBY GAZED THROUGH the lead-light window at the picturesque palace grounds. The pastel-hued roses were in full bloom, the immaculately trimmed deep green hedges were framing the flower beds, white pebbles along the meandering pathways glistening in the early morning sun. And the sky above was azure and cloudless. It truly was fairy-tale-perfect, and so much more than Libby could have dreamed possible for her Easter wedding day.

The test results had arrived the day before and they were negative for Daniel. He had not inherited the mutated gene from his father, which meant that Billy was not at risk either, but Libby had agreed to marry Daniel without knowing. When he had proposed, on the condition they wait for the test results, she had insisted the wedding was going ahead no matter what the report said. She would love him for better or worse and she meant it. Daniel and Billy had bonded almost immediately upon meeting. They were like two peas in a pod. Billy was his father's son in more ways than just good looks and Libby knew they would never spend another day apart.

'Only a few more buttons and I'll be finished,' her mother said softly as she poked her head around her daughter's waist and smiled at her reflection in the antique oval mirror. 'You truly look like a princess. Just beautiful. You do know it's almost guaranteed your father will cry when he sees you.'

'I don't think so. Dad's not like that. I've never seen him cry,' Libby replied, with a hint of disbelief creasing her forehead.

'He cries on the inside. You can't see it but he cries and today there will be tears of happiness that might just overflow,' her mother said, returning to her original position as she looped closed the last few pearl buttons that secured the back of the stunning silk wedding dress. It had been made by a team of local seamstresses and had taken three weeks to complete. It was a tradition for all the royal brides of Chezlovinka.

The ornate ivory gown skimmed her shoulders, with a band of antique lace from Daniel's mother's wedding dress. The sleeves were of the same lace and they had been cut to a point that framed her manicured hands. The bodice was cinched at the waist with a low back and a long train.

The door suddenly burst open.

'Oh, my Lord, you look like a princess!' Bradley pronounced as he came rushing to the bride. He was dressed in an emerald-green-and-black-striped silk suit with lapel embellishments. Libby thought momentarily it was a little more Broadway than Chezlovinka but that was Bradley. She smiled as he grew closer, his arms outstretched. He was never understated. He was loud and fun and she wouldn't change a thing about him. He was her best friend and that would never change.

'That's just what I told her,' Libby's mother said, and she spun around with her hand outstretched not unlike a traffic controller. 'But absolutely no hugging, you two. You'll crush the dress.'

Bradley stopped in mid-step. 'Of course. I wouldn't dream of crushing that divine creation.'

Libby laughed. 'A little hug would be fine.'

The two embraced cautiously before Bradley stepped back. 'Honestly, Libby, you look like a china doll, a red-haired china-doll bride. You couldn't look more beautiful. Or more perfect.'

'That's so sweet of you.'

'Honey, it's the truth and I hope Daniel knows just how lucky he is—'

'He does,' a little voice interrupted.

All three turned to see Billy standing in the doorway. 'Daddy did my bow-tie this morning and he told me that he is the luckiest man in the world because he's got Mommy and me for ever and ever.'

Libby felt her eyes begin to fill with tears.

'Oh, no, you don't,' Bradley cut in. 'You can't cry, you'll ruin your make-up. No smudgy bride on my watch.'

Libby laughed and Bradley pulled his crisp handkerchief from his top pocket and gently mopped the tears at risk of staining her cheeks.

'What would I do without you?'

'I have no clue and Tom and I will be visiting this quaint part of the world often so you won't have to find out,' he said with a smile. 'Plus, you have to come back to visit us at least twice a year. We can't have Billy losing his accent. I just won't allow him to grow up with some posh European way of talking that I can't understand.'

The door opened and an immaculately dressed woman with an earpiece entered. She smiled but it was a somewhat strained smile and her general demeanour, behind her chestnut chignon, midnight-blue suit and nude stilettos, was that of a woman on a mission.

'Bradley, this is our wedding planner, Simone,' Libby said.

'Lovely to meet you,' Bradley replied, after giving her the once-over and approving of her outfit. 'I'm guessing it's time to get this show on the road.'

'The groom and the wedding party are in place, along with the rest of the royal family and international guests,' Simone announced with a heavy Western European accent. 'You are only a five-minute carriage ride to the church but you need to leave now.'

'This is it, and the last time I can call you Libby McDonald,' Bradley said, as he carefully lowered the antique lace veil. 'Next time we meet, you will be Your Royal Highness.'

Libby leaned in as the veil dropped over her face. 'You will always call me Libby, that won't change. Not ever.'

* * *

Moments later, after the short trip in the open carriage to the two-hundred-year-old church, Libby stepped down onto the red carpet and smiled at the crowd as the bridesmaids hurriedly smoothed her dress and straightened her veil and ten-foot train.

'You look stunning, Libby. You're a true princess,' Georgie whispered, then took her position as Maid of Honour.

There were gasps of joy and waves from the people who had gathered there, many of whom had been waiting since dawn to see their beautiful new princess. She waved and smiled back at them with genuine joy filling her heart. She should have been overwhelmed but knowing that Daniel would soon be her husband and finally they would be the family she had always wanted lessened her nerves.

Despite Simone's exemplary planning, protocol had been thrown to the wind when it came to Billy. He had travelled in the carriage with Libby and his grandfather but once they'd come to a stop he had jumped down, patted the large grey horse nearest to him then raced inside the church on his own. It had been planned that one of the groomsmen would walk Billy to Daniel, who was waiting at the altar, but Billy was far too excited to see his father.

Georgie and the other bridesmaids and flower girls did follow protocol and walked on cue to the church doors and as the organ music began they walked in step inside and out of Libby's view.

'Well, it looks like there's a whole lot of pretty important people who've travelled a long way to see you,' Libby's father said as he patted her hand. 'We'd better not keep them waiting. Not sure if they can still behead for such a thing in this part of the world, but let's not find out.'

Libby giggled from behind the veil and, taking her father's arm, walked inside the church. Organ music filled the church, the beautifully dressed guests were seated in pews decorated with white roses and lily of the valley, but Libby saw none of it. All she could see was the most handsome man in the world turn to see her. Her soul mate, the love of her life, and the father of Billy and their future children was waiting at the altar, dressed in his red military attire and a smile that spoke to her heart. It told her everything she needed to know. Prince Daniel Dimosa was the man of her dreams and she was about to become his wife.

As she took her first step down the aisle, she read his lips as he said, 'I love you, Libby.'

Libby's heart was bursting with happiness. She had found her prince and her happily ever after.

* * * * *